SCOUT'S HONOR

HENRY VOGEL

Published in the United States of America by Rampant Loon Press, an imprint of Rampant Loon Media LLC, P.O. Box 111, Lake Elmo, Minnesota 55042. "Rampant Loon Press" and the Rampant Loon colophon are trademarks of Rampant Loon Media LLC.

www.rampantloonmedia.com

Cover art by Jeff Doten.

ISBN: 978-1-938834-41-7 (ebook)

ISBN: 978-1-938834-42-4 (print)

First publication: April 2014

For every person who has gazed up at the stars
and wondered, "What if?"

ASTEROID FIELD

"Wormhole ejection in one minute," warned the nav computer.

"Acknowledged," I said. "Computer, verify the emergency message drone is receiving the sensor data feed and is ready to launch."

"Verified," the computer responded.

For the remaining few seconds, the computer was silent, leaving me to mentally prepare for as many wormhole endpoint hazards as possible. Unfortunately, there are some hazards you simply can't prepare for—exiting into the middle of an asteroid field is the worst one of those.

The collision alert began wailing at the same time my scout ship emerged from the wormhole.

"Computer, launch the drone," I said, firing thrusters to avoid an asteroid larger than my ship.

"Drone launched," responded the computer in its unflappable, calm voice.

"Tell me when the drone enters the wormhole," I said, diving under a rock the size of an aircar.

"Unable to comply," said the computer as I spun the ship starboard as fast as possible, barely sliding between two large asteroids.

"Unable to comply?" I asked. "Why?"

"Ship's sensors are blocked by the asteroid field," the computer told me.

"Acknowledged," I said for the hundredth time since my ship had first entered the wormhole.

Then I tuned out the computer and worked on staying alive. I almost made it out of the field without taking major damage, too. With the edge of the field only a short distance away, my scout ship shuddered from an impact. It was a small asteroid, just a few meters across, but it was more than large enough to breach the hull and damage internal systems. With air rushing out of the breach, my ship tumbled out of the asteroid field.

A planet lay just beneath me, far closer than one should be to an asteroid field. Out of control, the scout ship plunged toward the planet below.

THE AIRSHIP

The ship spun and tumbled dizzily as the air in the cabin shrieked, leaking out into space. Strapped tightly into the pilot seat, there was nothing I could do to repair the hole in the side of the ship. Even if I were free to move, I wouldn't survive more than a few seconds of being tossed about the cabin.

"Abandon ship protocol initiated," the computer said inside my head, broadcasting directly to my implant to overcome the screams of my dying ship.

The pilot's seat dropped through the deck and into the escape pod, plugging itself into the control interface. The interface showed green and the escape pod launched itself from the ship. As it plunged toward the unknown planet, I had my first real chance to look around. I hadn't been in an asteroid field. The wormhole exit was inside a planetary ring.

My sightseeing was cut short when sensor readings started coming in. The readings cut off as the pod hit the atmosphere, but what I'd read looked promising. The planet should support human life, at least.

I held the pod's flight steady until it completed entry into the atmosphere, absently noted a fuel leak alert, then issued the command to deploy the wings and stabilizer. The expected whirring of the wings unfolding was replaced by a harsh grinding. That sound told me there was a major problem before the lights started flashing. I guess the asteroid impact had managed to damage more than just the escape pod's fuel tank. Fortunately, the designers had taken many possibilities into account when designing the escape pod, including fuel leaks and wing damage. The escape pod was a lifting body and could glide without the wings. More or less.

I worked the controls, slowly changing the angle of descent, waiting for the pod to begin generating some lift. At two hundred meters, with the pod finally leveling out, I found my glide path blocked. A primitive airship floated dead ahead. Instinctively, I dove beneath it—and the escape pod lost most of its lift.

The ground rushed up, ready to crush me.

CRASH LANDING

My eyes slid over the controls, desperately searching for a way to create some more lift. Almost on their own, my eyes slid back to the fuel gauge. The remaining fuel barely registered on the gauge, but it might be enough to fire the maneuvering thrusters for a few seconds. If I could nudge the escape pod toward level flight and add some forward momentum, maybe...

I fired the thrusters.

One second.

Two seconds.

Three-

The thrusters cut out, all of the fuel depleted. But the escape pod was moving forward again and slowly generating lift. I wrestled with the controls, trying to make the escape pod glide by force of will alone. The pod was leveling out slowly but it was losing altitude much too quickly for comfort. I yanked back on the controls, forcing the pod to nose up. If the nose of the pod hit first, it would cartwheel across the landscape, leaving pieces of itself—and me—scattered all over the place.

With a bone-jarring impact, the back half of the pod hit the ground. Skipped into the air. Hit the ground again. Skipped again. And suddenly, there was a small lake below me. The pod splashed into it and bobbed to a stop. With all the holes and rips in the pod's skin, I didn't think the pod would stay afloat for long. Slapping the harness release, I grabbed the standard issue survival pack. The pod was sinking even faster than I'd hoped, so I popped the canopy and dove into the water.

I struck out toward the shore, about fifty meters away. A couple of minutes later, I staggered out of the water. Scrub brush grew up around the water. Beyond that little ring of greenery stretched desert as far as I could see. From the other side of the little lake, I could hear something moving through the bushes. It sounded like something big, like something I didn't want to meet. Keeping an eye behind me, I struck out toward the desert.

At that moment, a man's voice cried out in pain and then cut off abruptly. The cry was followed by a woman's scream.

A DESPERATE FIGHT

Dripping from my swim to shore and clutching the emergency pack, I looked about for the source of the scream. A couple of hundred meters away, I saw a jumble of boulders. Now that I was alert to it, I could also hear the sounds of fighting going on beyond it—weapons clashing and voices shouting.

I ran to the boulders and quickly scrambled to the top. Below me, battle whirled between two human warriors, struggling to defend their position with swords, and about two dozen spear-thrusting wild...men? No, they were humanoid but not human, having squat, powerful bodies, blue skin, and sloping foreheads. Blood darkened the ground around bodies from both sides.

The warriors were backed against the boulders, forming a wall of flashing steel between the humanoids and a beautiful, raven-haired young woman. She moved restlessly behind her two guards, her sword poised to slash out should a humanoid come within her reach. As I took in the scene, one of her guards fell, a spear thrust completely through him. Even dying, the man found the strength to drive his sword into the stomach of the blue man who had thrust the spear. There was no scream from the young woman this time as she stepped forward to take his place.

Reflexively, I reached into the survival pack and grabbed the Onesie. The techs and quartermasters called it a Single-Shot Solar-Rechargeable Survival Blaster. All the scouts simply called it a Onesie because one shot per charge was all you got. Holding the Onesie over my head, I gave a wordless bellow. The fighting stopped as everyone turned their attention to me.

Brandishing the gun, knowing none could understand me, I yelled at the humanoids, "Leave or face the wrath of the Sky Wizard!" Then I fired the Onesie at the ground before the blue men..

I guess the blue men didn't like wizards. With guttural shouts, they charged at me.

BATTLING THE BLUE MEN

Dropping the survival pack and the discharged Onesie—it would be hours before it could be fired again—I leapt to meet the charging blue men. *Boost*, I thought to my implant. Instantly, the implant flooded my body with adrenaline. Unless I could finish the fight quickly—not likely, given the odds— I'd pay a serious price for the abuse Boost put on a human body. But if I was going to save the man and the beautiful young woman, I was going to need all the strength and speed of Boost.

With adrenaline raging through my veins, I moved among the wild blue men so fast that none of them could land a solid hit. The blue men crowded around me, plunging their spears into each other as I dodged and wove among them. I felt no pain from the scrapes and cuts I picked up. When the blue men got too close, I used my enhanced strength to lift one of my attackers above my head and wielded him as a club, beating his fellows from around me.

Tossing aside the broken body, I scooped up a fallen spear and continued my dance of death among them. As the bodies of the blue men piled up behind me, the blue men still fighting with the man and the young woman realized the greater danger lay at their backs. They couldn't seem to decide whether to turn to face me or try to overwhelm the other two humans. Their hesitation doomed them, as the remaining guard shifted from defense to attack. We drove toward each other, cutting down all who stood before us.

Even as my spear plunged into the last of the blue men, I was turning to see if the man or young woman were wounded. My eyes met the flashing, green eyes of the young woman. She spoke in a language my implant's translator had not yet interpreted. I assumed it was some form of thanks.

I smiled and replied, "No problem. Glad I was able to help."

Having far exceeded Boost safety limits, my implant read the relaxation in my posture. Determining I was now safe, the implant cut off Boost. The adrenaline stopped flowing and pain from my abused muscles slammed into me. I fell into darkness even before I fell to the ground.

THE AIRSHIP RETURNS

"Highness, let me bind this man," a gruff voice said. "He could be one of the raiders."

"He's not, Rob," said a lilting, female voice. "We'd never have escaped if he was. He's the best fighter I've ever seen."

"More reason to bind him," said the gruff voice. "We can always choose to release him after he wakes up. We certainly cannot bind him *after* he is awake."

The two must have been talking the whole time I was out. The translator in my implant had analyzed their language and was translating for me. Now that I was conscious, it would begin teaching me the full language, but I already had some words.

"He right," I said, sitting up and finally getting a good look at the man and young woman.

The man was probably in his mid-forties and looked like an experienced soldier. He had drawn his sword the second I spoke, moving with lethal grace.

The young woman was perhaps twenty, only a few years younger than me, with a tall, slender beauty that was breathtaking to behold. She was pointing my discharged Onesie at me.

"Who are you?" asked Rob. "Where do you come from?"

"Not easy to tell," I said. "Learn talk take time."

"That's another thing, Highness-" Rob began, cutting off as a shadow passed over us.

Looking up, I saw the airship I had nearly rammed. It was sailing a few hundred meters above us. I was drawing breath to shout to them when the princess gasped in dismay.

"Well, Highness, now we learn whose side this young man is on," Rob growled. "The raiders have found us."

RAIDERS

"Raiders chase you?" I asked, wishing my implant could imprint their language more quickly.

"Yes. We escaped yesterday," Rob replied. "Now, those who sacrificed themselves so we could do so have died in vain."

"No," I said, grabbing the survival pack. Above us, the airship was clearly venting gas to lose altitude.

"Ha," I said, pulling a large, thin cloth from the pack. "Safe now."

"Are you mad?" asked the princess, holding out the Onesie, "Drop the blanket and use this weapon to destroy them!"

I checked the Onesie's solar recharging unit. I'd been out longer than I thought because the gun would soon have enough charge to fire. But it would not be soon enough. Wrapping myself in the cloth, I dropped to the ground. "What see?"

The princess gasped, "Rob, did he just turn into a rock?"

"Well, Highness" Rob considered, "he *looks* like a rock."

"Chameleon cloth," I said, using the Terran term. I handed the cloth to Rob, "You two, under. Hide."

"What of you?" the princess asked as Rob wrapped the cloth around them.

"No room, Highness," I said. "I distract."

I handed the Onesie back to the princess and pointed at the controls, "Green good. Red bad. Point. Press button."

Taking the gun, the young woman gave a brief nod. Rob wrapped the chameleon cloth around them and they blended into the terrain.

Ropes dropped from the airship as it neared the ground. I began running toward them, waving my arms as men began sliding down the ropes. Seconds later, I was surrounded, half a dozen sword points pricking my skin.

TALK OR DIE

"Where is the princess?" a voice asked as swords pressed in all around me.

"Princess?" I asked in return, trying hard to feign confusion.

A tall, broad-shouldered man stepped into view from the left. A very recent wound slashed down his right cheek.

"Do not try my patience," demanded scarred-face. "My men saw you with her mere moments ago."

"She princess?" I asked.

"Yes, idiot, she is a princess. And if you don't tell me where she went, I'm going to have my lads poke several big, nasty holes in you." He smiled warmly, "Now, talk or die."

I pointed almost directly at Rob and the princess, "Go that way."

"South? Farther into the desert?" Scarred-face laughed jovially, "The idiot thinks I'm a fellow fool. We go north. Prod the idiot along, boys."

The raiders took scarred-face at his word. Every couple of steps, one of them poked me in the back with his sword. Soon, I was hopping forward with every other step, trying to stay just out of reach of the prodding. This drew laughs aplenty as my captors turned it into a game.

The game kept them so distracted that they didn't notice the two meter drop off until I hopped over it and vanished from sight. Shouts rose behind me as I sprinted toward a nearby tumble of rocks. Nearly there, I looked back and was surprised to see the raiders had stopped chasing me.

As I spun back to look forward, I heard a deep-throated growl. Looking up, all I could see was twin rows of long, sharp teeth.

TAMMAR

The raiders backed away, muttering "tammar." The predator—for it could be nothing else—stood two meters tall at the shoulders and was five meters long. My choices weren't good ones; die on the tammar's fangs or Boost and probably die overtaxing my body. Probably dead was better than definitely dead. I prepared to Boost.

The sound of a fully charged Onesie cracked through the air. The tammar's head disappeared in a spray of blood. Turning, the raiders and I saw the princess holding the gun. She was already turning the gun on the raiders.

"Run. Now," she commanded. "Unless you want to end up like the tammar."

All but scarred-face broke and ran. He stared at the princess, a smile crossing his lips, then he turned and walked after his rapidly receding crew.

"Nice timing, Highness," I said, joining Rob and her. "I'm in your debt."

The two stared at me in shock. Quickly, it dawned on me what was wrong.

"You're wondering how I learned your language so quickly," I said. "It will take some explaining, most of which you'll probably find unbelievable."

"What little we know about you—especially this weapon—is already unbelievable," the princess said, handing me the Onesie.

Taking the gun, I said, "You realize your threat was empty, Highness?"

"The raiders did not know–" she paused. "I do not even know your name."

"I am David Rice, Scout First Class of the Terran Exploration Corps," I said, bowing. "Let's start walking and I will happily tell my story."

The princess looked to Rob. "Northeast, Highness. I spotted a trading outpost during our escape from the raiders."

Carrying only the provisions in the survival pack, we headed into the desert.

PRINCESS CALLAN

W e spoke little throughout the afternoon, moving too quickly to waste breath talking. At dusk, Rob slowed the pace.

"While we're hardly safe, Highness," he said, "following our trail will not be easy. Especially from an airship."

"Thank you, Rob," the princess replied. Turning to me, she said, "You promised us some unbelievable explanations, Scout First Class David Rice."

"First, please just call me David, Highness."

"Very well, David. This is Captain Robbill Vonsteader, captain of my personal guard. I am Her Royal Highness, Princess Callan Debah Lois Antrulta Ziliah Villas, daughter of His Royal Majesty, King Edwar of Mordan. You may continue to call me Highness, though Princess Callan is also correct."

"Thank you, Highness," my lips twitched up in a smile. "I'll start with the most relevant part of my story. I had never laid eyes on this planet, nor even knew it existed, until today..."

Princess Callan's eyes grew wide as I told of my wormhole exit and subsequent crash. "I told you I was a member of the Terran Exploration Corps. Terra is another planet, the original home of the human race. Thousands of years ago, humans began leaving

Terra to settle on other worlds. These colonists traveled the vast void of space, many of them spending decades in transit. Some of those ships left no record of their destination. Some of them wished to withdraw from human civilization entirely, so recorded false destinations. And some of the records have simply been lost. The Terran Exploration Corps was formed, in part, to look for those lost colonies." I paused briefly, "Colonies such as your planet.

"Do your cultures have myths and legends telling of a great journey, Highness? Perhaps something along the lines of ships crossing the Sea of Night? Considering my experience earlier today the tales probably end with many of the ships being cast upon rocks and very few of the brave travelers reaching the new land alive."

"Yes, David, we do have such tales. They're almost exactly as you describe," replied the princess. "In certain scholarly circles, there is hot debate concerning those stories. Some claim the stories are based on true events while others are certain the stories are merely attempts to explain our presence here on Aashla. You say those tales are true?"

"Yes, at least in part," I said. "Is Aashla what you call this planet?"

"Every schoolchild knows that, David," Princess Callan said. Looking into my eyes, she continued, "Yet I believe you did not."

"Thank you, Highness. I know it will require quite a leap of faith to believe my story," I said.

"Is there no way to bolster my faith in your story? You could just be an adventurer with a fanciful imagination or simply insane. Can you offer proof, as well, David?"

I held out the survival pack, "Highness, you've used my weapon, heard me learn your language in less than a day, hidden beneath the chameleon cloth, and watched me fight while Boosted. I can offer no more proof than that."

"What of this ship you crashed this morning?" Callan persisted.

"It sank into the small lake," I said. "Yes, I know that sounds very convenient for my story, but it is true."

"Highness, all of this is quite fascinating," said Rob in a tone that belied his words, "but we must find a defensible place to spend the night. The tammar you killed was drawn out in daylight by the scent of blood from our fight, but they usually hunt at night."

"Of course, Rob," Princess Callan said. "But if danger strikes, at least we have David and his astounding Boost."

"Highness," I said, "do not depend on that. Boosting places an incredible strain on my body. Using it again so soon could kill me."

The princess appeared shocked at my words. Rob, on the other hand, looked surprisingly satisfied. Perhaps he was happy to learn just how mortal I was.

A site was soon selected and camp established. We ate a meal of tasteless survival bars from the pack then settled in for the night, Rob taking first watch. It seemed as if I had only just closed my eyes when Rob's hand clamped over my mouth.

"Wake up but make no sound or sudden moves," he hissed.

I opened my eyes and instantly knew what was wrong. A long, black snake-like thing was coiled on the princess's chest. It had hundreds of tiny legs along its body and a single fang bared in its open mouth. The thing's head was raised and ready to strike. The princess lay still, her eyes so filled with terror that I knew this snake-thing's bite must be deadly.

THE DESERT CREATURE

I f the snake-thing was like Terran snakes, it was probably searching for warmth and found it on the princess's chest. Now aroused, it was nervous and looked likely to strike. Whatever we were going to do, it had to be done fast.

"Red or green?" I asked quietly.

"Red," Rob answered quietly, instantly knowing I referred to the Onesie. "This Boost of yours—does it make you faster?"

"Yes, but maybe not fast enough."

"But you must-" Rob began, breaking off as the snake-thing hissed and moved in agitation.

I waited, letting the creature settle a bit before answering, "I will. Now, give me your hat."

Without another word, Rob carefully handed me the hat to his guard's uniform. Slowly, I began moving the open end of the hat in front of the snake-thing. The thing swayed in agitation then struck at the princess—a fraction of a second *after* I Boosted. The creature's head plunged into the hat, its strike blocked. I grabbed it just below the head and pulled it off of the princess. Its legs wriggled disturbingly within my grip as I dragged it outside. Drawing his sword, Rob smoothly cut off its head.

Quiet sobs drew Rob back inside the tent to comfort the princess. I took up the watch in his place.

After a while, the sobs faded and, finally, were replaced by the deep, rhythmic breathing of sleep. When Rob looked outside, I motioned him back into the tent. The princess would feel safer if she awoke to a familiar face.

As dawn was breaking, I heard the raider's airship engine in the distance. Worse, I realized the airship was ahead of us. It was apparent the raiders knew of the outpost and knew it was our only hope for survival. They would be waiting for us when we arrived.

GIVING MY OATH

We broke camp immediately, hoping the outpost was close and we might reach it before the raiders could prepare for us.

"Highness, you know my story," I said, trying to distract her from the previous night's horror and from the raiders ahead of us, "but I know little of yours."

Rob gave a nod and she said, "Very well, David, it's not a complicated story.

"I was being escorted to my betrothal to Prince Rupor, heir to the throne of Tarteg. Ten airships of the Mordanian Navy escorted my own airship. Over unsettled lands, a large force of raiders surprised us. Three raider ships attacked my ship. When it was obvious all was lost, I ordered my men to surrender.

"The raiders locked us in one of their airship's holds and flew south. A few hours later, ten of my guards broke out of the hold. They attacked the raiders, sacrificing themselves as a distraction for the rest of us. In the confusion, Rob grounded the airship and we ran. Several hours later, you arrived."

"A harrowing tale, Highness," I said. "But why would the raiders come south? I would assume any ransom would be paid in the north."

"With her lineage and beauty," Rob said, "Princess Callan would fetch a very high price in the southern slave markets."

Slave markets? I knew primitive colonies had been known to revive the vile practice, but it was still shocking to hear.

Rob added, "I will die before allowing that to happen."

Unable to bear the thought of anyone—especially one so lively and lovely—being sold into slavery, I said, "As will I."

Rob stopped walking, "Will you swear to that, David?"

"Rob-" began the princess.

I interrupted, raising my right hand. "On my honor as a Scout First Class, I swear to protect and defend Princess Callan to the best of my ability, even at the cost of my life."

Rob smiled for the first time since I met him. "Nontraditional but quite satisfactory." He extended his hand. "Welcome to the Royal Guard, David."

"That was unnecessary, David," the princess said.

"Perhaps for you, Highness," I replied, "but it was essential to Rob."

Suddenly, a shout rang out. "The princess! She's over here."

The raiders had spotted us.

DAVID THE DISTRACTION

The shout was taken up by other raiders and quickly echoed all around the trading post.

I turned to Rob, "You two use the chameleon cloth to hide while I-"

"It's gone, David," Rob said. "Lost when we threw it off so the princess could shoot the tammar."

"All right," I said, "new plan. I'll lead the raiders on a merry chase while you and the princess make your way around the trading post to the raiders' airship. They know where we are and are intent on surrounding us quickly. That will take most of the crew, so their airship should be lightly guarded."

"Right," Rob nodded. "After we take the ship, we'll wait for you for two minutes."

"Cast off immediately," I said. "Her Highness's safety is all that matters. Do *not* wait for me."

Rob nodded but the princess disagreed. "No! We all escape together or-"

"Highness, there are a very few times when your royal guards may disregard your orders," Rob said. "This is one of them. Your safety is paramount."

The princess shook her head in disagreement but did not

argue. With that settled, I scuttled away from Rob and the princess. A moment later, I rose and dashed off in the direction opposite the path they would take. My appearance immediately drew another shout and the chase was on. I used rocks, bushes, low dunes, gullies, anything I could to pop in and out of sight. I couldn't draw the raiders off unless they saw me, but I couldn't give them too long a look or they'd realize they were chasing one person instead of three.

Perhaps a minute later, I came face to face with my first raider. I vaulted over a boulder and found him lurking behind it. I ducked his wild sword swing and ran him through with my own sword. He fell, screaming and twitching as life drained out of him. I popped up and ran out.

Behind me, someone shouted, "He killed Farley!"

Any raiders who hadn't been chasing me, would be after me now.

A moment later, I crested a small dune and saw the main building of the trading post before me. Gambling that all of the raiders were in the desert chasing me, I ran to it and threw open the door. Half a dozen raiders, led by scarred-face, stood within. They all had their swords drawn. Behind me, the raiders who had been chasing me charged up to the outpost.

I was surrounded by raiders. Again.

THE PLUNGING PRINCESS

I thought about Boosting, but knew I couldn't. I could always trigger Boost if things got desperate, but until the princess was safe, I had to save it to use in her defense. With raiders all around me and no chance to survive a fight, I chose the only direction available to me. Up. Jumping, I caught the edge of the low roof and had pulled myself onto the roof before the first raider could react.

It was a mistake.

I had a great view of the raider airship. It was on the far side of the building and just lifting off. Now that they were looking up, the raiders outside the building could see the same thing.

"The airship," rose the cry. "She's loose and floating away!"

Raiders ran for the lines hanging from the airship, even before scarred-face began shouting orders at them. I pounded across the roof, hoping to grab a line and climb to the deck ahead of the raiders. That wasn't going to happen. Some raiders must have been near the ship and they were already scrambling up the lines.

Glancing at the airship deck, I saw Rob holding off three raiders while the princess sawed away at a dangling line with her dagger. There was no way she could cut all of the lines before the first raiders reached the deck. I *had* to get aboard the airship soon or all was lost. Casting aside caution, I sprinted to the edge of the roof and leapt off, aiming for a line dangling from the airship's starboard side.

I just managed to catch the end of the line. Even as I began the long climb, I saw several raiders reach the deck of the airship. The princess saw them and shouted a warning to Rob. She also saw a raider heading toward the line I was using. Princess Callan ran to defend my line against the raider, pitting her dagger against his sword. She whirled, dodged, blocked, and then tripped. I was halfway up the line when she fell against the railing, overbalanced, and fell from the airship!

SAFE IN MY ARMS

The princess plunged toward me, her eyes wide with terror and locked on mine. Wrapping my legs around the rope, I lunged out to intercept her fall.

Boost!

Her flailing hands would have been impossible for me to catch without the added speed and strength of the Boost. I caught her wrist, grasping it with both hands, but her momentum dragged us both down the line. A scream tore from the princess's lips, but I tightened my legs around the line and our descent stopped.

I pulled her up, wishing I could take the time to comfort her. "Wrap your arms around my neck."

She was shaking from terror but, mastering it, did as I instructed. "Hold tight, Highness, we're going up very fast."

With Boosted strength and agility, I swarmed up the line faster than any monkey. The raider at the railing had just enough time to realize the princess hadn't fallen to her death before we leaped onto the deck. Grabbing his shirt, I threw him off the airship. I sat the princess down, well away from the rail, then drew my sword and raced to Rob's aid.

I crashed into the raiders around Rob like a human battering ram, knocking two more over the rail and sending the rest flying across the deck. Rob, whose back had been to our ascent, stared at me in astonished relief.

"Her Highness-" he began.

"She's safe," I said, pointing behind me. Then I attacked the remaining six raiders. They were better fighters than the blue men I'd fought earlier—could it have just been yesterday?—but I also had Rob at my side. In less than a minute, the last raider fell to the deck.

Pain slammed into me as the Boost cut off, but this time I remained conscious. That meant I was entirely awake and aware when the princess—the *betrothed* princess—flew into my arms and began kissing me passionately on the lips.

REBUKED

I received a lot of training in the Scout Academy. None of it had covered my situation. When the princess's lips locked on mine, all rational thought fled, leaving instinct to take over. Placing my hand on the small of the princess's back, I pulled her close and returned the kiss. Enthusiastically.

"Ahem!"

We jumped apart like a couple of preteens caught necking in school, our eyes downcast and unable to meet Rob's stern gaze.

"Highness, go to the stern of the airship," Rob ordered.

The princess bristled at his tone, "Rob, you will not-"

"*Callan*, do as I say."

Chastised, she stalked aft.

Trying to head off the coming rebuke, I said, "Rob, I -"

"*Silence, boy,*" hissed Rob. "Less than an hour ago, you took an oath to protect the princess with your life. That includes protecting her from herself and her infatuations. That includes protecting her from your base instincts. *Do you understand?*"

"Yes, sir!"

His gaze bored into mine.. Satisfied, he unbent slightly. "Many men develop strong feelings for those they guard, David, especially when their charge is a beautiful young woman. Burying those feelings is your duty."

"It will not happen again, sir."

He nodded and seemed to be satisfied. "Now, can that...thing...in your head teach you how to fly this airship?"

I checked and, to my surprise, my implant did have information on piloting airships. As Rob headed aft toward the princess, I concentrated on the airship controls. I tried very hard to ignore the discussion taking place at the stern, but it sounded like the "protectee" version of the speech Rob had just given to me.

I needed to figure out how to gain altitude so we could reach the prevailing winds. That meant forward speed and the right angle on the ailerons to generate lift beyond that provided by the gas envelope. A little experimentation with the controls showed me what I could do from the wheel. I'd have to set the ailerons by hand, but I could pilot the ship well enough to get the princess back to her country.

Looking up from the controls, I spotted a dark smudge on the horizon. Grabbing my survival pack, that Rob had brought aboard, I took out the binoculars and trained them on the smudge. Ice lanced through my gut as the smudge came into focus.

A sandstorm stretched across the horizon, bearing down on us.

THE SANDSTORM

The sandstorm drew visibly closer in the few seconds I watched through the binoculars. We needed a new course and a lot more speed or the storm would have us.

"Rob," I called as I turned the ship away from the onrushing storm.

Turning from the princess, brows drawing down in irritation at the interruption, he said, "Not now–"

"Sandstorm! It's closing fast."

Rob was standing next to me seconds later. I handed him the binoculars as I turned the ship away from the sandstorm.

"Look through—," I began.

"We have similar devices," Rob said, lifting the binoculars to his eyes. "Though none are so sharp or powerful as these."

Studying the storm, Rob added, "It appears you can fly this ship."

"Not well enough to fly through the storm."

"Can we outrun it?" he asked.

"Probably not, but..." I turned to the princess, "Highness, take the wheel and hold it steady. I need to show Rob something."

She took the wheel without a question. I led Rob to the engine room, below.

"Have you ever worked a steam engine?" I asked.

"Yes, years ago," he replied.

"If we're going to have a chance of outrunning the storm, I'll need as much steam as you can get me," I told him. "Even if the storm catches us, having our own power may help."

As Rob began feeding wood to the fire, I added, "I'll send the princess below. It will be safer for her down here, out of the storm."

The wind had risen considerably in the short time I'd been below. Taking the wheel, I told the princess to go below.

She gave me a sudden smile, "You kiss quite well, David. The woman who marries you will be a lucky woman, indeed. For her sake, whoever she is, do be careful."

She turned and went below, leaving me to wonder exactly what she meant.

Rob built up the steam quickly, powering the twin propellers to spin ever faster. Still, I doubted we could outrun the storm. It bore down on us, gaining no matter what I did with the airship's controls.

I fought the buffeting wind, scanning the desert for any place where we could land and take cover. Then the storm blotted out the sun and sand scoured the deck.

The storm was upon us.

ABANDON SHIP

The storm swept over the airship and visibility was cut to nothing. I wasn't sure if I could see the bow or was half imagining it through the swirling sand. I fought to keep us from being driven into the ground or being turned sideways to tumble keel over gas envelope. The ship danced on the wind, beyond my ability to exert much control over its course. I sensed more than saw a dune rise up before the ship and just managed to keep us from plowing into it. The airship's keel still scraped the top of the dune, jarring the ship.

Time vanished, leaving me with no idea how long I'd been fighting the storm. My implant told me it was mere minutes, but I felt as if it had been hours. Flayed by sand, my body taut with tension, I was on the ragged edge of exhaustion. So I did not notice that Rob was beside me until he grabbed my arm.

He was shouting but I could barely hear him over the storm, "Boiler pressure is rising too fast. Probably a clogged pipe, but there's no way to fix it before it blows. Not in this storm."

I shouted back. "You and the princess will have to abandon ship. I'll get us down close to the ground so you can jump safely."

Rob nodded. He understood there was no other way to insure the princess's safety.

"I'll blow the whistle when it's time for you to jump," I said.

"What of you, lad?"

Instead of answering, I shouted, "I'll find you once the storm passes."

"I don't doubt it for a moment, David." Though it was obvious he *did* doubt it. Clapping my shoulder, he went below.

I took the ship down until I was sure I saw ground beneath the airship, then blew the steam whistle long and loudly. Its wail rose above the roar of the storm and I hoped Rob and the princess had jumped safely. As the wind drove the ship up again, I heard the steam whistling again. For a moment, I thought the whistle had jammed, then I realized the sound was coming from below—from the boiler.

I dashed for the ship's railing but was too late. With a roar, the boiler exploded.

TRAPPED

I drifted on the edge of consciousness, struggling to stay away from it. For I knew pain lurked behind consciousness and I could not have one without the other. Better to float in mental limbo for a while longer, hoping the pain would get tired of waiting for me and go away.

"*David!*"

The voice reached to me, below the surface of consciousness, and pulled me upward. That voice meant something to me. It meant beautiful green eyes. It meant long raven hair. It meant a warm smile and a tall, slender body. It meant *Callan*. I came fully awake at the thought of her. With awareness came the pain, but also remembrance. Raiders. Escapes. The kiss. Her betrothal. My oath.

"*David!*"

I tried to respond but managed only a soft cough. Then I struggled to stand and found I could not. Prying my eyes open, I discovered I was buried under the debris from the wrecked airship—wood, rope, cloth. Experimenting, I found I could move one of my arms. I knocked on the wood as hard as I could.

"David? Is that you?"

I knocked again.

"Rob! He's over here. He's buried under the wreckage."

Footsteps approached and then a pair of eyes peered at me through an opening in the debris.

"I'm glad to see you made it, lad," said Rob. "I can't see much of you in there except your eyes, but I assume the rest of you is intact."

His arm reached as far into the opening as possible, "Here's a water skin. Drink, clear your throat, and conserve your strength. It's going to take a while for us to free you."

The water tasted heavenly and the sound of debris being cleared was music to my ears. And it lasted all of two minutes.

"Rob?" The princess sounded worried. "There are horses coming."

It was silent for a few seconds then Rob cursed.

"What is it?" I managed to croak.

Rob's reply was flat and chilling. "Slavers."

MARTIN BANE

"How far away are the slavers? Do you think they've seen you?" I asked.

"Half a mile, maybe," Rob answered, "and I doubt they've seen us yet. We should blend in with the wreckage at that distance."

"Then hide," I said. My implant told me half a mile was almost a kilometer. They could get clear if they left now. "When they get close, I'll call out for help. Maybe they won't look for anyone else if they think I'm alone. At the very least, they'll have fewer men searching for you."

Rob stood, "It's the best chance we've got, Highness. Let's go."

The princess's voice drifted down to me, "Take care, David."

I heard the two of them scrambling away followed by silence. Finally, I heard the riders approaching.

"Help!" I called. "I'm trapped under the wreckage."

The light was blocked and then voices began jabbering in a language new to me. It wasn't surprising, but it would make things more difficult until my implant could analyze and imprint the new language.

More jabbering came from the slavers, followed by the sounds of wreckage being moved. With horses to help drag larger, heavier pieces of the wreck, it only took fifteen minutes before hands were pulling me out. I put on my best grateful smile.

"I am so happy to see you! I'd never have gotten out on my own," I cried. "How can I ever thank you?"

The shadow of a rider fell across me.

"You can start by telling us where the princess is," said scarred-face. "And then you can explain what happened to my airship."

Time for plan B.

Boost! I snatched a sword from the slaver closest to me and leapt for scarred-face. All I had to do was take him hostage. That ought to be easy enough.

Moving impossibly quickly, scarred-face grabbed my wrist and threw me several meters from his horse. Then, he somersaulted off his horse and drew his sword, all before landing lightly on his feet.

Dropping Boost, I rolled to my feet and stared at him, "Who-"

"Ah, forgive my poor manners. We have not been properly introduced," scarred-face said, bowing. "I am Martin Bane, Scout Second Class of the Terran Exploration Corps."

CAPTURED

"What-?" I began, but my thoughts stalled there. I tried again, "Why-?"

"You have quite a fascinating array of conversational gambits, my good man," Bane said, "but let's get back to the one important issue. Where is Princess Callan?"

That got through to me. "The princess and her bodyguard jumped off your airship during the sandstorm. Sand had clogged the boiler and pressure was getting dangerously high. I'd planned to follow them, but never could drive the ship close enough to the ground again."

"You flew my ship into a sandstorm?" Bane asked.

"No, I tried to run from it. The storm was too fast." I waved my hand toward the wreckage, "You can see the end result. But the princess is probably miles away from here."

Bane didn't believe me and called to his men, "Keep searching around the wreck. I'm sure those two are around here somewhere."

His men probably would find the princess and Rob unless I could distract them another time. Boosting once again, I leapt onto Bane's horse, slapping its flanks with the flat of my sword.

Bane was caught by surprise, but his men ran for their own horses. The chase was on!

If I could get a dune between myself and the airship wreck, it would give Rob and the princess a chance to slip away from the site. I just had to keep the slavers busy for a few minutes.

The slavers were much better riders than me and came close to cutting me off before I topped the nearest dune. Two riders were racing to block me and it looked like they were going to succeed. Trusting to Boosted reflexes, I stood in the saddle, dove over them, and rolled down the far side of the dune. Whooping, the slavers chased after me.

At the bottom of the dune, I prepared to die fighting the slavers. Instead, they stayed well away from me and began twirling weighted ropes. Three riders threw their ropes at the same time. I jumped over one and ducked another, but the third wrapped tightly around my legs. Three more ropes followed, pinning my arms. Struggling against the ropes, I toppled over and could only watch as Bane strode over to me.

"We're going to find the princess," he said. "and you'll get to watch while she's sold at auction. Then I'll sell *you* at auction, too, and use the money I make to replace my airship."

Grinning, Bane bashed me on the head with his sword pommel and all went black.

SACRIFICE FOR NAUGHT

I awoke lying down, my hands and feet tied to a bed frame. Bane was there, watching me, a thoughtful expression on his face.

"How old are you, kid? Twenty-four?" he asked.

"Not quite."

"You must be the youngest Scout First Class ever," he said.

"Nope," I replied.

"Second youngest, then," Bane said. "And not by much, I'd bet."

"What makes you think I'm a Scout First Class?" I asked.

"There's no Master Scout with you," he said. "And since you're not mourning one's death, it seems obvious you were exploring alone. You can only explore alone if you're a Scout First Class."

"Does that mean your Master Scout—the one who was completing your training—is dead?"

"Yeah. We were hit by an asteroid right after our exit from the wormhole. She was killed instantly."

"How did you end up..." I wasn't sure how to complete that sentence.

"Like this? Raider, kidnapper, slaver?" he asked. "It's a long story and we don't have time for it."

"Have you got a pressing engagement somewhere?" I asked.

He shrugged and said, "I crash landed a day's walk from Morda, the Mordanian capital. I managed to walk to the city, but ended up in the worst part of the city. My implant picked up the gutter language spoken there, so I even sounded like one of the dregs of society. I went into the wrong bar, got into the wrong fight, Boosted at the wrong time, and killed a couple of thugs.

"That's usually not a big deal in the poorest quarters, but there was extra security because of a certain princess's fifth birthday. Someone had tried to celebrate Her Highness's fourth birthday by kidnapping her, so the city guard was being extra careful this year. No one in the city knew who I was and I couldn't give an explanation they were willing to listen to.

"I even tried telling them the truth, but even I wouldn't have believed my story if I'd been in their place. I'd usually have gotten time doing hard labor, but someone decided to make an example of me. I was sentenced to hang. Instead of hanging, another prisoner and I escaped. I've been working the other side of the law ever since."

He stood, "Some of us aren't lucky enough to crash on top of royalty, Wonder Boy. Some of us get stuck dealing with the seedy underbelly of a primitive civilization."

Bane was about to add something when the door flew open. Rob and the princess were pushed into the room by grinning slavers. My sacrifice had been for nothing.

THE MYTHICAL HERO

Bane beamed at his men. "Well done, lads. Who gets the bonus for making the capture?"

"No one," Rob growled. "We came here on our own."

"You did *what*?" I said

Bane nodded toward me, "I'm with Wonder Boy on this one. Why would you give yourself up after you worked so hard to give us the slip?"

"Because we saw an army of trogs coming this way," answered Rob. "There are hundreds of them. Distasteful as it may be, this trading post was our only hope for survival."

Bane's expression grew serious and he said, "Rouse the men! Get spotters on the rooftops." Turning to Rob, "How much time have we got?"

"Thirty minutes, if you're lucky," he replied. "Highness, please release David."

"No, princess," Bane barked. "Wonder Boy is-"

"The best warrior here," Rob interrupted. "Let him help us."

Bane thought for a few seconds, nodded, then said, "Wonder Boy-"

"My name is David Rice," I said.

"Very well, Rice," Bane said, "give me your word of honor—as a Scout—that you will relinquish your sword to me after the battle."

I looked to Rob. He nodded.

"Yes, you have my word," I said.

As the princess untied my bonds, tears pooled in her eyes.

"Hey, Highness," I said, rubbing my wrists, "don't cry. We're going to get out of this alive, you know. Then we're going to escape from Martin Bane and get you home in time for your wedding."

Princess Callan wiped her eyes and tried to smile, "What makes you so sure of that, David?"

"I crossed the ocean of night and survived being cast upon the rocks," I said. "Then I found you in your most desperate hour. Isn't it obvious? I'm the mythical hero who rescues the beautiful princess."

The princess giggled, "But isn't the mythical hero supposed to marry the beautiful princess?"

"Shhh! Don't let Rob hear you say that," I said. "I don't want another lecture from him. These trogs—are they the blue men you were fighting when we met?"

Prince Callan nodded as I stood.

Bane said, "There are swords in the next room. Grab one." Then he asked, "Who has the Onesie? It could be useful."

"It's gone, lost when the boiler exploded" I said. "Besides, firing the Onesie just makes trogs mad."

"You'll forgive me if I don't believe you," Bane said. "I'll have to search-"

A shout interrupted him, "To arms! The trogs are here!"

Bane shot a look at Rob, "You said thirty minutes."

"I guess you weren't lucky," Rob shot back, as we grabbed swords and ran from the building.

As I'd expected, we were back at the trading post. From all around us, spears waving, blue figures charged toward us.

INTO THE CELLAR

I took one look at the trog horde and knew they would overrun us with ease. Turning to Bane, I asked, "How well do you know this outpost?"

"What difference does it make?" Bane almost shouted.

"Does it have a storm cellar or a root cellar?" I demanded. "Some place underground with a single entrance?"

Comprehension dawned on Bane, "Yes."

Turning to his men, he ordered, "Recall everyone. We're going into the cellar."

We ran into the main building as his men spread word of the retreat. There was a trap door in one corner. It opened into a storage cellar, just as I'd hoped. I sent Rob and the princess into the cellar first.

"What of you, David?" asked the princess, concern in her eyes and voice.

"One of us guards you and one of us guards the entrance. Don't worry, I'll come down once everyone else is safely below," I told her, offering a confident smile.

After they had moved out of sight below, Bane gave me a sly grin. "Maybe Wonder Boy is the right nickname for you after all.

Less than two days on the planet and you've already got the beautiful princess panting after you. You *are* a fast worker."

"Shut up," I growled.

I was saved further jibes as Bane's men began piling into the building. They wasted no time in jumping into the cellar. None of them showed a bit of concern for me as I waited for everyone to enter the cellar. By the time the last of Bane's men had jumped into the cellar, the howling of the trogs was deafening. Bane leapt down, leaving me to climb down the ladder and shut the trap door. I stayed on the ladder, sword in hand, ready to defend the door.

The doors to the building crashed open and heavy feet trod across the floor. A minute dragged past as we listened to the trogs searching the trading post. Then footsteps stopped above the trap door. It was flung open and a trog thrust his spear at me.

Boost!

I grabbed the spear and pulled. The trog tumbled to the floor below and Bane's men fell upon him. Above, two more trogs took his place.

Our battle for survival had begun.

DEFENSE OF THE DOOR

Adrenaline blazed through my veins, giving me the strength and speed I needed to kill quickly. Our precarious position gave me the incentive to kill ruthlessly. Unless I could convince the trogs their attack wasn't worth the cost, I would fall. I'd suffer Boost Burnout or dodge left when I should have dodged right, and that would be it for me—and everyone else. The trogs would take the ladder when I fell. Once they controlled it, trogs could drop straight into the cellar. After that, it wouldn't take long for them to crush the remaining humans. There was no way around the terrible math of our predicament. If the trogs were willing to spend enough lives and take enough time, they would slaughter us all—even the princess.

Blood and snarls and screams filled my senses and time no longer had any meaning to me. I'd killed seventeen trogs and dragged four more into head-first dives to the cellar floor. Those four were killed before they could stand, but one of those trogs had still managed to kill two men despite lying on the floor. My implant said I'd been Boosting for nine minutes, three times longer than any known record. How long could I keep this up before I burned out?

Guttural shouting from above rose over the din of battle. A

powerful voice cut through the shouts. Silence fell and the attacks ceased. I overrode my implant's safety protocols before it could turn off Boost. I knew I'd black out immediately after Boost shut down and I couldn't afford that. Besides, the attack could be renewed at any time and I had to be ready.

In the silence, we heard the sound of an airship engine above the trading post. Airmen could attack the trogs from above, never having to come within range of their spears. We waited to hear the cries of dying trogs. And we waited in vain. The engine droned on, fading as the airship passed overhead without stopping.

"Huuuuuumans," the powerful voice called. The faces below me went white, terrified by something I didn't understand.

"No warrior death for you," the voice continued. "You die, like beasts."

A trog slammed the trap door shut then we heard them piling heavy objects on top of it. A few moments later, the smell of smoke wafted down to us. The trogs had set fire to the building.

I dropped the override on my implant's safety protocols and it shut down Boost. I had just enough time to feel my heart stop beating before darkness overwhelmed me.

GOOD FORM

I woke up. That was a surprise. My aching body hadn't killed me after all. I was lying on a dirt floor and, despite stiff, aching muscles, I felt comfortable. It was as if something was right in my world. Warm liquid splashed on my face. I opened my eyes and looked into the princess's tear-filled eyes. And now I knew what felt so right—my head lay cradled in the princess's lap. I smiled.

"Hi," I croaked.

Princess Callan's lovely green eyes focused and she gasped, "David? You're awake!"

A dazzling smile lit her face, drawing an answering smile from me. I would give anything, *do* anything, to keep that smile in place.

Rob and Bane stepped into view, towering over us both.

"Welcome back, lad," Rob said, smiling. "Good form, not dying."

Bane's eyes flicked to the princess, "Did you know your heart stopped when you stopped Boosting?"

I nodded. I'd remember that feeling for the rest of my life.

Bane continued, "My men performed a little CPR—something I teach everyone in my crew—while I fashioned a makeshift defibrillator using the Onesie. That's why you're still alive."

Bane held up the disassembled Onesie. "I don't know where she managed to hide it," his eyes roamed appreciatively over the princess's formfitting clothing, "but she did."

"After your heart started again, he said you shouldn't try to Boost again anytime soon," the princess said. "On this subject, at least, the raider and I agree."

"As you wish," I replied. Then another thought entered my head. It seems odd now, but at the time I felt as if it was the most important question in the world. Maybe it was my brain overreacting to my near death experience, but I asked, "Why did everyone look so scared when the trog leader spoke?"

The three of them exchanged glances, perhaps wondering if I had suffered some sort of brain damage.

"Trogs have never spoken human languages," Rob said. "It's generally assumed they're too stupid to learn it."

"Trogs have never organized an army, either. A hunting party is about the best they can do," Bane added. "Perhaps their leader is some kind of trog genius."

"When we get out of here, we've got to warn the northern countries," Rob said. "It's only a two day march to the border of Mordan."

"No, we don't," Bane said. "We've got a deal. You go to the Southern slave markets and you behave along the way. Just like your princess promised."

"*What?*" I cried.

"He was going to let you die, David," the princess whispered. "I couldn't let that happen. I promised him nothing he wasn't going to get, anyway. They outnumber us ten to one. We were going to the slave markets one way or the other. At least this way, you're alive."

"You don't think I destroyed that Onesie out of the supposed goodness of my-" Bane said, stopping as a deep thrumming sound reached us.

The airship was back!

PRINCE RAOUL

We all looked up, as if we could see through the floor to the airship droning above us. No one spoke as our ears strained to catch any change in the engine's roar. We heard the engine shut down.

Minutes dragged by and we tried to make the airship crew find us by our force of will. Then we heard a thump from above. It was followed by another, and another after that. The sound of wood scraping against wood carried down to us. The debris of the trading post was being cleared.

"Hey!" I shouted. "We're in the cellar."

Two dozen voices roared as everyone else took up the shout. The sounds from above stopped, then renewed. More and more thumping and scraping came from above. More airmen were joining in the work.

Half an hour later, the sounds from above ceased. Footsteps stalked to the trap door. With the creak of hinges, the trap door opened and too-bright light burst upon us. Uniformed men began dropping into the cellar, each with a sword drawn and ready for action.

Princess Callan gasped, "Tartegian airmen."

"Your betrothed?" I asked.

Nodding, she rose to her feet, in the process transforming from the frightened young woman who had cradled my head into royalty. The regal bearing of a princess settled over her like a second skin. One of the airmen spotted her instantly.

"Prince Raoul," the airman called. "She's here."

"Raoul?" I asked.

"Rupor's younger half-brother," Rob answered.

More men dropped into the cellar, forming a wall of swords between Bane's men and the trap door. They were followed by a compact, energetic man about my own age.

"Callan?" he called.

"I'm here, Raoul," she said. "But beware, most of these men are raiders and slavers."

"I only want the princess, her companions, and your leader," Raoul said, his eyes sweeping the ranks of men. "If the rest of you surrender, you have my word I'll release you when we leave."

Bane must have Boosted, because he leapt over the line of Tartegian airmen and had a dagger at Raoul's throat before anyone could react.

"Coincidentally, I also only want the princess, her companions, and *your* leader," Bane said. "Surrender or your prince dies."

THE SPARE PRINCE

Prince Raoul's men milled about, uncertain of what to do. Martin Bane pressed his dagger against their prince's throat, nicking it.

"Do as I say or you'll be wearing the blood of your prince," Bane growled.

"No," Raoul gasped. "Don't risk our future queen's life. Not for the Spare Prince."

Bane laughed, "Bravely spoken, Spare Prince, but your men know what Mommy will do to them if they let you die. There's not a man among them foolish enough to cross the queen."

I filed 'Spare Prince' away for later and whispered, "There's got to be something we can do. If I Boost, maybe I can-"

"No," Callan responded. "I will not allow you to kill yourself for no reason."

"She's right, lad," Rob added. "The raider captain has your same abilities. If Boosting didn't kill you, he'd kill Raoul before you got close."

Within the circle of airmen, Prince Raoul stretched his neck, as if inviting Bane to slit it, then said, "Men, I order you to disregard any threat to my life and rescue Princess Callan."

"Belay that," commanded a voice from above. "If necessary,

another woman can be found for Prince Rupor, but we cannot find another prince of the realm. Mister Bane, name your terms."

"No, Admiral Hamlan," said Raoul. "No terms. No surrender. The men must-"

"The men must follow my orders, Your Highness," said the admiral. "Mister Bane, I will accede to the following terms. You, your men, and your captives may leave unhindered, provided my men are unharmed and you release the prince safely."

"Agreed," said Bane, "though I've thought of one addition to my demands. I will also take your airship."

"You may take the airship's skiff, Mister Bane," Hamlan said. "along with my guarantee of safe passage."

"That's quite generous of you, Admiral," Bane said, "but how many men will your skiff carry?"

"A dozen."

"I have rather more than a dozen men with me," Bane said. "I don't suppose you have a spare skiff or two?"

"No, I do not," Hamlan said.

"And do you have a spare prince, Admiral?" Bane said. He flashed a grin at his men.

"Very amusing, Mister Bane," Hamlan said.

"I thought not," Bane said. "And that's why I'll be taking your airship."

The admiral sighed, "You leave me little choice. We have an accord."

Keeping his dagger at Prince Raoul's throat, Bane backed into a corner, then ordered the Tartegian airmen to ascend the ladder. Bane's men followed, took the weapons from the airmen, and established a perimeter around the trap door.

"After you, princess," Bane said. "Your guards will remain here, of course."

"I will not-" Rob began.

"I gave my word, Rob," Princess Callan said. "You will not gainsay it."

"Aren't you forgetting something?" I asked Bane. "You said you wanted to sell me at auction, also."

"That was when I needed to replace my ship. Thanks to the Spare Prince, I have a brand new Tartegian warship," Bane replied. "Princess, ascend if you please?"

Princess Callan gave Rob and me one last look, then climbed the ladder. Raoul and Bane followed behind her.

The trap door slammed shut and, with thumping and scraping, debris was piled atop it. The airship engines roared to life, then faded as Bane flew away with the princess.

MISJUDGING RAOUL

A s soon as the airship's engine faded away, we heard men begin clearing the debris from the trap door.

I asked Rob, "What's the deal with this 'Spare Prince' nickname of Raoul's?"

"Later," Rob said. "We have more important things to do."

"No, we don't," I said. "We can't make plans until we know the situation above. So tell me about Prince Raoul. It may be important, later."

"I suppose it might, at that," Rob said. "Do you recall me saying Raoul is Rupor's half-brother?"

"Yes."

"When Prince Rupor was three, his mother died of a debilitating illness," Rob said. "The Tartegian nobles gave their king little time to grieve before pushing him to remarry. For the good of the kingdom, of course. King Damon gave in, marrying the first suitable woman presented to him.

"Next, the nobles pressed Damon to have another child, to insure the succession if something happened to Prince Rupor. Again, he gave in. When Raoul was born, Damon is said to have told his advisors, 'Congratulations, you have your spare prince.' Alas for Raoul, the name stuck."

I contemplated what it would be like growing up with such a nickname as the last of the debris was cleared from the trapdoor. It was opened and we climbed out. A Tartegian airman led us to Admiral Hamlan.

Rob asked, "Where is Prince Raoul?"

"Still on the airship," Hamlan sighed.

"Bane lied? Shocking," I said.

"Actually, Bane didn't lie," Hamlan said. "He allowed the prince to slide down a line just as the airship was getting underway. A crewman called for Bane and he walked away just as the prince began sliding. I guess Bane assumed His Highness would continue down the rope. Unseen by those aboard, Raoul slipped into an open porthole."

"This is the man all of you call the Spare Prince?" I asked.

"Perhaps all of Tarteg has misjudged Raoul," mused Hamlan, "not least his father."

"It was bravely done," said Rob, "but Prince Raoul is only one man. He won't be able to take over the airship alone. Are there more Tartegian airships in the area?"

Hamlan shook his head, "No, our southern squadron is scattered, searching for your princess. Nor are there any animals to ride. I fear we'll have to walk out of here."

"If you'll loan me a dozen of your men, Admiral, we can build a vehicle," I said. "Rob and I can be pursuing Bane in just a few hours."

Hamlan looked at Rob, who said, "If David says he can do it, I believe him."

"Very well, but some of my men must ride with you," Hamlan said.

"There won't be room," I said. "Besides, you need to find a way to warn people about the trog army."

"Hardly an army, and they've been dealt with," Hamlan responded.

"You dealt with several hundred trogs?" Rob asked.

"Several hundred?" scoffed Hamlan. "More like two dozen."

"Their leader must have kept them under cover when the airship flew over the trading post the first time," I said. "Rob, fill him in while I get the men started."

I left Rob explaining the trog situation to the admiral and called the airmen together.

"Listen carefully," I said, and watched their eyes grow wide as I explained my plan.

It *had* to work. If it didn't, the princess would be lost to me forever.

SAND SCHOONER

Three hours later, Admiral Hamlan looked at the result of our work and said to Rob, "He's crazy, right?"

"Not at all," Rob replied with confidence. "I'm sure this... *What* is it, David?"

"I've been calling it a sand schooner," I said. "The wide wheels will allow it to ride on top of the sand and the sail will catch this desert wind and drive it forward."

"But that is hardly more than a frame with wheels, two seats, and a sail," protested Hamlan.

"It was important to keep the weight down, sir," I said. "And, with the wind that's been blowing for the last couple of days, it'll be fast."

Rob and I climbed into the seats on the frame, the sail flapping loosely in the wind. I trimmed the sail, it filled with wind, and the sand schooner began to roll. The airmen raised a cheer as the admiral shook his head in disbelief.

"Good luck," Hamlan called. "and do bring my prince back in one piece."

The sand schooner cleared the ruined buildings of the trading post and, catching the full force of the wind, picked up speed quickly.

Rob said, "Incredible! It *does* work."

I cocked an eyebrow at him.

"You didn't think I would express doubts in front of Tartegians, did you?" he asked.

Soon, the sand schooner was sailing along at a steady twenty to twenty-five kilometers per hour. At that speed, we might not gain on Bane's airship, but wouldn't lose much ground, either. I taught Rob how to handle the schooner, allowing us to take shifts at the helm and avoid having to stop for rest.

Racing over the dunes, we sailed beyond the sunset and into the night, steering as much by instinct as by moonlight and the light from the planetary ring. A few hours past midnight, our instincts failed us.

We crested a huge dune only to find the other side dropped off like a cliff. The sand schooner flew over the edge and plunged toward the sand a hundred meters below us.

A RICH MAN'S TOY

The sand schooner arching through the air was fun for the second it took for my brain to remind me that we were falling. Neither Boosting nor training would get us out of this alive. Rob and I shared a helpless look. I was just considering if the sail could be a makeshift parachute when the sand schooner hit something soft—an airship's gas envelope.

"Jump!" we both said as the schooner began to slide down the envelope's side.

Rob managed to catch a line but my hands found only smooth fabric. I scrabbled to find something to grab—and only found it when Rob swung his leg to me. No longer sliding, I was able to grab a line of my own and we began to climb down to the deck below. My heart didn't stop hammering until, half a minute later, my feet were firmly planted on the airship's deck.

The moonlight illuminated a utilitarian, but still stylish, deck.

"This airship seems a bit small," I said.

Rob said. "I've seen the like before. It's a rich man's toy, nothing more."

"Oh, it's much more than that!" protested a voice. "But it's a bit of a toy, as well."

A large man, rounded with rich living and slowed by advancing age, stepped into view. His voice carried the tone of command, but there was an undertone of humor.

"Now, how did two gentlemen such as yourselves board an airborne ship?" he asked. Before either of us could answer, he said, "Come below. I rather expect this will be a long story."

He walked aft. Rob and I followed. We stepped on lines lying on the deck, quite out of place on the otherwise neatly arrayed airship. My brain raised the alarm too late. A net rose up around us, leaving us dangling from a boom. A smaller man rushed out of hiding and shoved the boom over the airship's side railing.

The old man spoke, "Oh dear, I have forgotten my manners and caught you in a net. I'll have my manservant release you immediately. Do enjoy your fall."

TRISTAN AGRILLA

"Kill us if you must," I said, "but then you will be responsible for rescuing the princess."

"A princess! This gets better and better," said the older man. "Let me guess, she's been kidnapped and is on her way to the slave markets in Beloren?"

"Sir, were our swords drawn when you confronted us?" I asked.

"No," admitted the man.

"Did we reach for our swords or offer any threats when you discovered us?"

"Again, no," the man said.

"That's not exactly typical raider behavior, is it?" I pressed.

"True," the man said. "But why did you board my airship? Even better, *how* did you board my airship?"

"That story is even more improbable than our kidnapped, slave market-bound princess," I replied.

The man gazed at me for a moment, then said, "Pull them back over the deck, Nist, but don't release them."

With the deck beneath us again, the older man looked into my eyes. "Is there really a kidnapped princess?"

I met his gaze, "Yes. We're pledged to her service."

"I suppose she's radiantly beautiful, as well?" he asked.

"I've traveled quite extensively," I said, "and have never met her equal."

"And you're in love with her," he stated.

"How could I not be?" I replied.

The man nodded slowly, "Release them, Nist. I *must* hear this story."

"Hear it you shall," Rob said, "but could we bring up the steam and set course for Beloren? Those who hold Her Highness are several hours ahead of us."

"Quite right, my good man," the man said. "Nist, it's time we found out just how fast the *Pauline* can go. Full steam! Full power! Full speed!"

A grin creased Nist's face, "At once, master!"

"Master?" Rob frowned.

"That's just Nist's little joke," the man said. "My late wife, after whom this ship is named, and I bought him when he was quite young. We freed him and then adopted him. Even so, he always called us 'master' and 'mistress.' It always drove my wife to distraction.

"Allow me to introduce myself," he continued, leading us below. "I am Tristan Agrilla."

Below deck, Rob introduced us and then asked me to tell our story. Tristan's eyes widened when I told him where I came from, but he didn't interrupt. The ship had crossed the desert and the sun was rising before I finished.

Tristan turned to Rob, "Do you believe his story?"

"I've seen him do amazing things. If anything, the lad has been too modest describing his actions," Rob said. "Her Highness believes him, that is good enough for me."

"Master," Nist called from the deck, "we're approaching the city of Beloren."

Returning to the deck, we saw a huge city rising out of fertile plains. Hundreds of airships swarmed about the city.

How could we hope to find Princess Callan amid that teeming mass of people?

BEAUTY NEVER PASSES UNNOTICED

I gave voice to my concern, "How are we going to find the princess in a city that large?"

Tristan said, "Young people are so predictable—quick to anger, quick to love, quick to despair. And slow to think."

Rob barked a laugh, "So true, my friend. I assume you have a plan for finding Her Highness?"

"I *always* have a plan," exclaimed Tristan.

Nist added, "Sometimes, his plans even work."

"Bah. Ignore him, gentlemen," growled Tristan. "You told me this Martin Bane is flying a Tartegian naval airship, correct?"

I nodded.

"Finding it will be simplicity itself," smiled Tristan. "There are only two docks in the city capable of handling such a large ship. One is in the warehouse district and of no interest. The other, my friends, is near the slave markets."

Nist piloted the *Pauline* deftly through the airship traffic toward a dock on the far side of the city. Even before we docked, Rob spotted Bane's ship at the dock. We had found his ship, but there was no activity on its deck. It was obvious Bane was no longer aboard.

I leaned against the airship's railing and hung my head. Tristan clapped me on the back. "Fear not, my boy. We'll find your princess. The raiders will have had to escort her to the slave market and beauty such as you describe never passes unnoticed."

After docking, we left Nist with the airship and climbed down to the street. Tristan spoke with various acquaintances before setting off toward a central market.

"Your princess was brought this way no more than two hours ago," Tristan told us. "It appears you did not exaggerate her beauty, David. Her passage brought business to a standstill. Finding her won't be a problem, though getting her away from the sellers will be another matter."

That's when I spied Bane ahead of us. "Maybe not," I said. "I'll bet Bane would give her to us in exchange for his own life."

I began pushing my way through the crowd toward him, planning how best to take him. I was only a couple of meters away from him when one of his men rushed up.

"The prince and princess," he gasped. "They've escaped."

"Imagine that," said Bane, taking the news quite calmly.

"You don't understand, captain. During the escape, the prince led the princess into the old sewers beneath the city," said the crewman.

Bane's face drained of color, "That idiot! I warned-. Gather as many of the crew as you can and meet me at the Market Street square. Hurry! There's a chance they're still alive."

BANE, AGAIN

Grabbing Bane's shoulder, I spun him around, "There's a chance they'll still be alive? What does that mean?"

Bane's eyes went wide, "Rice? How did you get here?"

"There's no time for that," Rob exclaimed joining me. "Answer the man's question."

Bane said, "The old sewers beneath the city are home to the most violent dregs of Beloren. The city guard only go down there in the most dire of emergencies. Then they go with at least a full squad, preferably three. The tunnel rats don't like outsiders and have nasty ways of dealing with those they catch. That's where the Spare Prince has dragged your princess."

Bane continued, "I've already summoned my men. We're going after them."

I didn't ask why, though I wondered. "We're coming with you."

"Suit yourself," Bane shrugged. "Just remember who's in command."

Tristan said, "That sounds quite exciting and dangerous, but an old man like me would just slow you down. What aid can I give from above ground?"

Bane was busy issuing orders to another crewman and paying

no attention to us. I said quietly, "Can you gather armed men you trust? We may need to take the prince and princess from Bane when we return."

If we return.

"You can count on me, my boy," Tristan said, turning away.

"We'll wait for my men at the sewer entrance," Bane said. "Come on."

Bane set a fast pace through the market, but many people greeted Bane by name as he passed. I realized that he was a well-regarded businessman in Beloren. Rob and I would have to be careful if we were forced into a confrontation with him.

Moments later, we stood in a narrow alley, staring down into a dark hole. I wondered how long we would have to wait—how long we could afford to wait—for Bane's men. When the answer came, I didn't like it. Guttural voices roared up from below.

"That's not good," Bane said.

"That tears it," I said.

Without another word, I descended into the darkness.

INTO THE TUNNELS

I slid down the ladder and dropped to the tunnel floor. There were widely spaced torches giving off just enough light to see by. Not waiting for Rob, I ran off toward the roaring voices. There wasn't a person to be seen in the tunnels, not even guards, until I was close to the source of the roaring.

The cheering crowd was deafening, but another sound rose above it—a sound that made my blood run cold. It was the cry of a tammar, the huge, fanged beast I had faced in the desert. A human screamed in terror, then in pain, and then was silenced. The cheering grew, crested, then returned to a steady roar.

I came to a branch in the tunnel and stopped to listen. The tunnels echoed with the sounds, but I thought the source of the sound came from the right. Glancing back as I sprinted into the right branch, I saw Rob was close behind me. The tunnel bent to the right and, ahead, opened out into a larger, far better lit room.

The entrance to the room was guarded by an ill-dressed man holding a sword. The guard wasn't paying attention to the tunnel. He was craning his neck, looking into the room. The noise from the crowd covered any sounds I was making. Lowering my shoulder, I charged.

The guard must have sensed something because he turned at

the last moment. His eyes widened and then I crashed into him. The guard flew backward, his face contorting in terror and his arms flailing. Then he fell into a large opening in the floor and dropped, screaming, to the floor several meters below. He landed next to the tammar.

The tammar wore a leather harness with a rope fastened to it. The other end of the rope was tied to an iron ring driven into the floor. Screaming people thronged a couple of meters beyond the limit of the rope. More iron rings were driven into the ceiling of this upper room. Ropes were tied to several of the rings. Two of the ropes hung down into the tammar pit and had mangled corpses tied to them.

In the pit, the guard attempted to scuttle away from the tammar. I heard the guard scream as I turned my attention to the upper room. A large man stood across the opening from me, shock written on his face. Princess Callan and Prince Raoul stood next to him, each tied like the corpses below. I couldn't risk leaping across the opening. If I landed wrong or the man blocked me, I could fall into the pit. I started running around the opening to the princess and prince. The large man grinned, grabbed the princess, and shoved her into the opening. Terror filled her lovely face as she plunged toward certain death.

THE TAMMAR PIT

Without hesitation, I jumped after the plunging princess.

The tammar crouched over the body of the guard, ready to pounce again. The creature had not eaten any of its kills. These tunnel rats had obviously trained it to kill for pleasure—theirs and its. The tammar had locked its gaze on Callan, but its eyes shifted to me when I landed. Rising from its latest kill, the tammar looked between Callan and me. It decided I was the more dangerous prey and turned toward Callan. I shouted and waved, trying to draw the tammar's attention away from the princess..

Boosted, I knew I could kill the tammar. But after my extended battle with the trogs at the trading post, I didn't know what another Boost would do to me. With Callan's life on the line, I couldn't take that kind of risk. Normal human strength and reflexes would have to be sufficient.

Rob dropped to the floor behind the tammar as it slowly stalked toward us. At least I wouldn't be fighting alone. The crowd had gone silent at the change in the program, so I had no trouble hearing Rob's command.

"Keep it away from Her Highness," he called, hacking at the rope tying the tammar to the iron ring.

Tied, the tammar was only a threat to those in the pit. Loose, it could be the distraction we needed to escape. As Rob finished cutting the rope, the tammar crouched, ready to pounce on Callan. I roared a challenge and charged, but the creature ignored me. Rob grabbed the end of the rope and hauled on it with all his might. The tammar was pulled up onto its hind legs, unable to pounce. I reached the tammar and attacked. My sword sliced across its chest. The tammar roared in pain and spun away, searching for easier prey. It bounded at Rob, who still held the rope in his hands.

The tammar's claws slashed and Rob fell. The tammar kept going, leaping into the crowd of tunnel rats. Screams erupted as the crowd scrambled to get away from the wrath of the tammar. I cut the princess's bonds and we rushed to Rob. The cries of the crowd and the tammar faded to nothing when I reached Rob. The wounds were mortal and Rob knew it.

"Do something!" cried Callan, tears streaming.

"There's nothing to be done, Highness," Rob gasped. "You know it's true."

She turned to me, "There must be something you can do!"

I shook my head, "I'm sorry, Highness."

"You're the last of the princess's guard, lad. Take my sword," Rob said. "Use it always in her defense."

I nodded, taking his sword. Rob pulled Callan close and spoke softly into her ear. Louder, he said, "I love you like a daughter..."

Then the light faded from his eyes.

I WON'T LEAVE HIM

I tore my gaze from Rob's body, looking around the pit as Princess Callan wept. Echoing through the tunnels, I could hear the cry of the tammar and the screams of the tunnel rats scrambling to escape the beast. Listening to the panicked screams, I felt the tammar was dealing a kind of savage justice to the tunnel rats. Not one of them remained around the pit. It was time to make our escape.

I said, "Highness, come on. We've got to get out of here."

Cradling Rob's head and still sobbing, the princess shook her head.

"Highness... Callan, he gave his life for you," I said. "If we don't go now, his sacrifice will have been for nothing."

"I won't leave him in these awful tunnels, to have his body abused by the wretches who live down here," she said.

I sensed motion behind me and leaped to my feet, Rob's sword ready. Prince Raoul, his hands still tied, had managed to find a way to slide down the rope.

"Could I trouble you for a little help?" he said, holding out his hands.

I cut his bonds, saying, "I need you to carry Rob's body. I'm going to have to carry Her Highness and she won't leave without him."

A look of irritation flashed across Raoul's face. Perhaps he didn't like commoners giving him orders or perhaps he would have preferred to carry the princess, but he lifted Rob's body over his shoulder and I gathered Callan in my arms.

"We need to hurry," he said. "I'm pretty sure I saw one of Bane's men approaching the room as I was sliding down."

I nodded and set off in a direction I thought would lead to a way up. We ran, dodging panicked tunnel rats along the way. The tammar's cries receded as we ran, giving me one less thing to worry about. I made several wrong turns and we dodged three groups of tunnel rats—all armed and grim-faced—before finding a tunnel that sloped up. Forty meters further, it intersected with the wide tunnel Rob and I had run through bare minutes and an entire lifetime ago.

A few minutes later, we reached the ladder up to the alley. It took some encouragement, but I got Callan to climb the ladder. I took Rob's body from Raoul, sending him up next. I followed as quickly as my burden would allow. Seconds later, I was blinking in the comparatively bright light of the alley.

"It sounds as if you made quite an impression down there," said a familiar voice. "And you managed to fetch my property along the way. Well done."

Bane and his crew blocked our way to the street.

A DARING ESCAPE

With the exit to the street blocked by Bane's men, our only hope was to head deeper into the alley.

"Run!" I said.

I heaved Rob's body at the crowd of men then ran off after Callan and Raoul. Her Highness might not approve, but Rob would have understood and approved. Even in death, his body was helping to guard the princess. The few seconds the raiders spent disentangling themselves from Rob could be the difference between capture and escape.

We dodged and dashed down the winding alley, but there were no branches, no side alleys, and no way out to the street. Rounding a bend, we found ourselves at a dead end. Walls rose up to the sides and ahead of us. But a set of stairs also rose up on the outside wall of one of the buildings.

"Take the stairs," I called. "Climb to the roof."

Raoul pulled Callan up the stairs behind him. I came up more slowly, ready to turn and fight if necessary. Behind us, Bane's crew charged around the bend and into the dead end. The narrow stairs slowed them down, as the men pushed and shoved, trying to be first up the stairs. We reached the roof a couple of flights ahead of our pursuers, but there my slim, final hope was dashed. There was no way down to the street. The building across the street was too far away for us to jump to it. The adjacent buildings were taller than our building, with no windows in the side walls. We were trapped.

"I'll hold them here," I said, taking position at the stairs. "Maybe there's a drain pipe on the front of the building that you can use to climb down."

"Wait, look up there," Raoul said, pointing.

A huge cargo airship moved slowly over us, a single line dangling to within a few meters of the roof. Sweeping Callan up in my arms, I lifted her toward the rope.

"Grab the rope and climb, Highness," I said.

As she did, I cupped my hands, "You next, Prince Raoul."

Raoul stepped into my hands and I lifted him. He caught the rope easily, but the airship was moving very slowly. With nothing to stop them, Bane's men might be able to catch onto the rope and recapture the princess and prince.

"Come on, David," Callan said. "Jump."

I called, "I have to stay and slow down Bane and his men. Drop down to the next roof and go to the docks. Find the airship *Pauline* in slip fifty-seven. They're friends and will get you home safely."

Bane's men rushed onto the roof, spreading out before me. I drew my sword, roared in challenge, and charged across the roof to meet them.

RESPECT

I expected some kind of answering challenge from Bane's men. Instead of advancing to meet my attack, they hung back, casting nervous looks between themselves. Maybe they were remembering my single-handed defense of the trap door against the trogs and didn't want to face me in a fight. If so, good. A few seconds of hesitation was all I wanted. In those few seconds, the prince and princess would be carried clear of the roof and make good on their escape.

One man plucked up the courage to come to meet me. Steel rang as our blades crossed, then Bane's voice rang out. "Stand down and stand aside."

Relieved, the crewman lowered his sword and stepped back. Bane stepped onto the roof. To my surprise, he cradled Rob's body in his arms. Rob's blood was staining his rich clothes, but the raider captain didn't seem to care.

"You dropped this," he said, gently laying Rob's body down at my feet. His eyes met mine, "I want you to know that I had true respect for him."

"As did I," I said, wondering what game Bane was playing now.

Bane saw my wariness and said, "You've nothing more to fear

from me and my men. I've done what I was contracted to do. In truth, because of you I've ended up doing far more than that."

"Contracted? You mean someone hired you to kidnap Princess Callan?" I asked.

"You have no idea how hard it is to get raider airships to work together. Without guaranteed payment, it's almost impossible," he said. "Of course, if I'd known you were going to fall from the sky, wreck my airship, and nearly wreck my plan, I'd have charged double. You have been one big thorn in my side from the moment you first appeared."

"Who hired you? They've got to have deep pockets if they could afford to hire so many raiders at one time."

"Oh no, there's no chance I'll tell you that, Rice," Bane said. "Clients expect secrecy and pay well to get it. If you want to know who hired me, figure it out for yourself."

Glancing past me, Bane asked, "Didn't your plan involve the prince and princess dropping onto a nearby roof?"

I spun about and saw the airship was fifty meters away. Its line was now hanging twenty meters above the tallest rooftops. The unknown airship was climbing to cruising altitude and the princess and prince were being carried away with it.

PURSUIT

The airship continued to climb as it passed over the city wall. It looked as if the princess and prince were shouting, trying to draw the attention of the airship's crew, but their cries were drowned out by the roar of the airship's big steam engines.

"Shouldn't you be running off to save them?" Bane asked.

"I will, but I want to make one thing clear. If anything happens to Rob's body..." I said.

"I told you, I'm finished with this passion play," Bane replied. "Go rescue your princess. Again. I'll see that Rob's body is properly prepared for a funeral."

Seeing the indecision written on my face, Bane added, "Scout's honor."

I looked into Bane's eyes and believed him. Looking over the edge of the roof, I spotted a drain pipe descending to street level. I climbed down the pipe and set off toward the docks at a run. As I entered the docks, I met Tristan leaving it, leading a band of armed men. His face creased in concern when he saw me.

"I gathered the men you requested as quickly as possible. Am I too late?" he asked.

"We've got to take off now," I said, slowing down but not stopping. "I'll explain in the air."

Tristan fell in behind me, lumbering through the crowds you can always find at a busy dock. His age and bulk took a toll. By the time we reached the *Pauline* he was red-faced and wheezing. I began casting off docking lines as Tristan stumbled aboard the airship.

"Nist, bring up the steam," I cried. "We've got an airship to catch."

Nist looked at Tristan, bent over at the waist and gasping to catch his breath. Tristan nodded and Nist began feeding the fire for the boiler.

Nist took us straight up while the pressure built. The little ship rose through the dockyard's traffic lanes and into the late afternoon sky. It had only been a few hours since we docked, but it seemed as if a lifetime had passed. A lifetime *had* passed for Rob.

The airship cleared the low altitude traffic and Nist set off in the direction I pointed. With the course set and Tristan's breathing returning to normal, I told them what had happened. They listened quietly, asking no questions. At the end, Tristan was briefly silent.

"I'm sorry, my boy. Rob struck me as a good man," he said. "For now, though, we have to concentrate on the living."

We said no more as the *Pauline* sped south in the wake of the cargo airship. The sun hung low on the horizon when we drew close enough to see the big airship clearly. The line still dangled from the ship, but the prince and princess were nowhere to be seen.

SLIPPING ABOARD

Nist maneuvered the *Pauline* close to the other airship and I hailed it. The reply sounded like the same language spoken by the slavers who had pulled me out of the airship wreckage a few days ago. I didn't understand a word of it, but Tristan did. He took over the discussion. After several minutes of calling back and forth between Tristan and the ship's captain, Tristan signaled Nist to fly away.

"What did he say?" I asked.

"He says neither he nor his crew saw anyone hanging on the line," Tristan said. "He claims the ship's envelope developed a large leak about an hour ago. That's not uncommon in an airship this size. The airship dropped close enough to the ground for the line to drag on it before the crew finished patching the leak. He suggests the prince and princess dropped off then."

"Do you believe him?" I asked.

Tristan said, "No... An airship that size shouldn't have lost so much altitude from a simple leak. Besides, the captain had all his answers ready to hand. He didn't ask his crew any questions but was quite certain about what the crew did *not* see. I'd say he's hiding something."

"Yes, and it's probably the prince and princess," I said. "Nist, turn the ship as if we're searching back along the airship's flight path. I want to give the captain the idea that we believed him. Once it's dark, we'll head back to that ship."

Two hours later, Nist guided the *Pauline* into position above the cargo airship's envelope. He held us steady, out of sight from the other airship's crew. The larger ship's engines drowned out our own smaller engine.

I looped a rope over my shoulder, testing to make sure it would remain secure without getting in my way. I tied another rope to the bow rail.

"When this line goes slack, I'll be safely on the envelope. Drop away and below the cargo airship's stern. When I've got the prince and princess, I'll flash a signal to you with a lantern. I'll lower them to you, starting with the princess" I said.

I slid down to the envelope, finding plenty of handholds within the lines criss-crossing it. I took my time climbing to the deck below, descending into shadows along the starboard rail. I hugged the rail, staying away from the ship's lanterns and avoiding the small night crew.

A few minutes later, I found my way below deck. I had taken but a few steps when a door opened and a crewman backed into the passageway. He was balancing a heavily laden food tray and backed right into me.

Keeping his eyes on the tray, the crewman muttered something at me. I grunted in return and stepped away from him. The crewman kept his concentration on the tray and headed aft. Only one person on the ship would receive such careful attention—the captain. I slipped after the crewman. At the end of the passageway, the crewman knocked on a door then opened it. The cabin beyond the door was brightly lit. Within, the captain laughed, pouring wine for another man.

The other man was Prince Raoul.

WHAT ABOUT RAOUL?

I ducked into a doorway and out of the light spilling from the cabin. Peering around the door frame, I watched as the crewman placed most of the food on the captain's table. The crewman lifted the tray again, speaking to the captain. I understood the words "princess" and "food." My implant had begun to translate the language. There was no doubt the remaining food was for Callan.

When the crewman left the captain's cabin, I followed. He went halfway up the same passage before unlocking a door and stepping inside. I trailed behind him and looked into the room. He placed the tray on the foot of a cot. Princess Callan lay upon the cot, her eyes looking everywhere except at the crewman. Callan's eyes went wide when I entered, a tight smile forming on her lips. Then she kicked the crewman in the stomach. The crewman stumbled back, gasping for breath. I clouted him on the back of the neck with the pommel of my sword, laying him out.

Callan rose from the cot and flowed into my arms. Her embrace was unlike the impetuous, passionate kiss a few days ago. It was simply one person seeking comfort from another.

Callan laid her head on my shoulder and whispered, "I knew you'd find me, David."

I held her briefly, stroking her hair, then said, "Highness, we-"

"Callan," she said. "In private, the captain of my personal guard calls me Callan."

"As you wish, Callan," I said. "But I don't know how much time we have before this crewman is missed. It can't take very long to deliver a couple of meals. We've got to get you out of here now."

"What about Raoul?" she asked. "I haven't seen him since a crewman took him away a few hours ago."

What about Raoul, indeed, I thought, but said, "I can't risk having them capture you again. Once you're safe, I'll come back and look for Raoul."

And I'll have a few questions for you when I find you, Raoul.

It's more difficult for two people to move unnoticed than it is for one. It took several minutes longer to slip to the stern of the airship than I had hoped. Hiding Callan in a particularly deep shadow, I took a lantern that was hanging nearby. Shuttering all but a sliver of the glass, I flashed a signal to the *Pauline*, flying almost invisible below us. I waited but a few seconds before I saw the flashing reply. I motioned for Callan to join me. She blanched when she saw me tying my rope to the ship's railing.

"I can't climb down a rope, David," she whispered. "My hands still ache from gripping the rope this afternoon."

I would never have risked having Callan simply slide down the rope and was already tying the rope into a sling, "Don't worry, all you'll have to do is sit in the sling while I lower you."

She was nodding when we were blinded as lanterns snapped open around us.

Drawing his sword, the captain said, "Our prize is trying to escape, boys!"

TRAPPED

With a start, I realized the captain had spoken in the princess's language. His accent was thick and his tone was flat, almost as if he had memorized the words. Did he speak the princess's language? There had been no indication of that when we had hailed him during the afternoon. I thought I had a way to find out if he did.

"Highness, I hope I can get out of this without a fight" I whispered. "If I'm wrong, I'll guard this rope while you slide down to the airship below. They are friends. Trust them."

Eyes wide, Callan nodded.

I turned to face the captain, my sword sheathed and my hands up. I smiled and said, "You filthy pack of airdogs, I'll kill you all."

The captain smiled back, then spoke to his crew. My implant picked out "princess" again, but I couldn't get anything else.

Shaking my head as if in dejection, I said, "Are you ready to die?"

It took the captain a moment to realize I had asked a question. The captain studied me for a moment and then nodded. That settled the question of language. The captain was trying to read my body language and had no idea what I was saying.

Prince Raoul burst from the shadows and charged at the captain. The crew just watched as Raoul dashed past them and wrestled the captain's sword from him. The captain raised his hands as Raoul put the sword against the captain's throat.

Raoul spoke in the captain's language, one arm sweeping across the watching crewmen. My implant translated "princess" and "guard" this time around. How I wished I knew what Raoul was saying. When Raoul finished speaking, everyone but the captain turned and scurried to the bow of the airship.

Raoul took a quick glance at me, "Do you have a plan for getting Her Highness off of this airship?"

Thrusting aside nagging doubts about Raoul, I said, "I've got an airship trailing just off the stern. They're waiting for me to lower the princess to them."

"Then go ahead and lower Her Highness to safety," Raoul said. "I'll keep this rabble at bay."

Whatever was going on, ensuring Callan's safety was paramount. I put her into the sling and lowered Callan to the *Pauline*. Below, Nist and Tristan pulled her onto the deck and I breathed a little easier.

Drawing my sword, I said, "You next, prince."

"What?" Raoul said. "No, you must go. The princess is still a long way from home and will need your protection during the journey."

"Princess Callan is safely aboard a fast airship and with people I trust," I said. "As a prince of a neighboring realm and Her Highness's future brother-in-law, your safety comes next."

Raoul was not pleased with my statement. He watched me for several seconds—seconds during which the captain just stood there—then, eyes flashing anger, Raoul dropped the captain's sword and stalked to the rope. A moment later a shout from below told me he was safely down.

I heard the twang of a bow string and a quarrel buried itself in the railing next to me. The crew had crossbows! While I was distracted by the near miss, the captain scooped up his sword and attacked. I dodged before realizing I was not the target of the captain's swing. His sword sliced right through my rope and it fell into the darkness.

I was trapped on the airship.

BOOST OR DIE

Dropping into a dueling stance, the captain grinned in triumph. A crossbow bolt plucked at my sleeve, the second near miss. Unless I could find some kind of cover, it was only a matter of time before the crew skewered me. There was nothing on the deck for me to hide behind, so I rushed for the only cover available—the captain. If I engaged the captain, his crew would have to hold their fire or risk hitting him. He stepped forward to meet me. I blocked his swing and my sword vibrated from the force of his blow. The captain was far stronger than he looked.

Could Raoul possibly have taken the sword from that iron grip without the captain's cooperation?

Seeing the effect of his blow, the captain pressed the attack and drove me backward across the deck. In the bow of the airship, half a dozen men held cocked and loaded crossbows. They were ready to fire if I strayed too far from the captain. The rest of the crew had grabbed boat hooks and belaying pins and, careful not to block the crossbowmen's aim, were walking toward the stern. It looked like everyone wanted in on the kill.

I had precious few heartbeats left before the crew reached us. If I didn't get away before then, I never would. Blocking another of the captain's mighty blows, I fell back against the starboard rail. The captain roared in triumph, believing my end was near. He was right. I was about to die and had nothing left to lose.

Boost!

Adrenaline surged through my veins and it was as if time slowed to a crawl. The captain attacked again, but this time I dodged the attack with ease. I flicked my sword past his guard and into his wrist. Blood flowed and the sword flew from his hand. Surprise and fear flashed in the captain's eyes. Spinning past him, I smacked the captain's head with the flat of my blade. The captain fell and the waiting crossbowmen could fire without fear of hitting the captain.

The crossbow quarrels flew at me in a ragged line. My sword flashed as I blocked the first five shots. Feeling like showing off, I snatched the last bolt from the air by hand. The crew stared, mouths agape, as I flipped the quarrel over the railing.

I sheathed my sword and gave a sweeping bow. The captain had trained his crew well, though. Their slack-jawed amazement at my theatrics broke and, belaying pins and boat hooks raised, they charged at me.

I could feel the Boost taking its toll—my system hadn't fully recovered from the fight with the trogs. I had to get off the airship. I sprinted to the point along the stern railing where the rope had been tied and dove into the darkness.

BACK TO BELOREN

Night-blinded by the lanterns on deck, I saw nothing but darkness below me. I had no way to judge how far out I'd jumped. Was it too far? Not far enough? Had the *Pauline* moved?

With a muted thump, I landed on the *Pauline's* envelope. Grabbing the first line I found, I squirmed and pulled until my body was underneath the line. Once I was secure from falling, I canceled Boost. I had Boosted for less than a minute, well under the safety limits. My muscles ached, but I didn't black out. It looked like I could begin counting on Boost again, within reason.

"David, that is you up there, isn't it?" called Princess Callan.

"Yes, it's me, Highness," I called back, "Please ask Nist to move the *Pauline* away from the other ship as fast as possible."

I watched the *Pauline* turn away from the larger craft. When we were clear of it and I was sure I wasn't suffering any after-effects of the Boost, I slid out from under the line and climbed toward the deck. A minute later, Callan and Raoul helped me onto the deck. Callan swept me into a tight hug.

"I knew you'd come for us, David," she said.

"It *is* the man's job, Callan," Raoul said, a frown making him look like a petulant child.

"Raoul is correct, Highness," I said. "And I expect my job to get a lot easier with you and His Highness safely aboard a friendly airship."

"Quite right, my boy," Tristan said. "It would be my honor to transport their Highnesses safely home."

Smoothing his face into a smile, Raoul said, "A generous offer, good sir. I will gladly accept, provided you agree to return Princess Callan to Mordan, first. Her parents must be worried sick about her."

"No, much as I want to go home, I can't yet," Callan said. Turning to Tristan, she continued, "I ask only that you return me to Beloren."

"Highness," I said, "why would you want to go back there?"

"Have you forgotten the trog army?" Callan asked. "They were but two days march from the Mordanian border. Our southern border was never heavily defended, as we rely on the desert to deter most invaders. With the navy mobilized to search for me, the border may be entirely undefended. Even now, the trogs could be attacking my people. I will not turn my back on them."

Tristan asked, "I understand your concern, Highness, but why stop in Beloren?"

Callan responded, "I need to speak with Martin Bane."

I NEED A FLEET

"Y
ou need what?" Raoul asked.

"To speak with Martin Bane," Callan repeated.

Raoul said, "But he kidnapped you."

"I know," Callan replied. "You may remember that I was there when Bane did it."

"Yes, but- but-" Raoul sputtered.

"He kidnapped me," Callan finished for Raoul. "Please stop repeating yourself. I have to look beyond the kidnapping, Raoul. The safety of my people outweighs everything Martin Bane has done."

"What can Bane do for you, Highness?" I asked.

"If I'm going to defend Mordan's southern border, I'll need a fleet," she replied. "Martin Bane can provide one."

"I don't know the man, so please pardon me for asking this, Highness," Tristan said. "What makes you think this Martin Bane can procure a fleet?"

"He's already done it," she said. "When we were trapped in the trading post cellar—you were still unconscious David—Bane described how *he* had hired the other raiders, how *he* had molded that rabble into a fleet, and how *he* had devised the tactics to separate my ship from the rest. The man would not shut up about it. At the time, it was really quite irritating. Now...

"I need a fleet as soon as humanly possible. There simply isn't time to look for other options," she continued. "So, Martin Bane it is."

"Will raiders be willing to fight trogs for you?" I asked.

"They're a rather mercenary lot, as I understand it. If the pay is right, we should be able to hire a fleet," she said.

"What of the Tartegian navy?" Raoul asked. "If this airship is as fast as we've been told, we could fly to the nearest base and I could lead a squadron of trained airmen against these trogs."

"No, Raoul," Callan said. "We cannot have the Tartegian navy in Mordan before the wedding. There's been animosity between our countries for too long. The Mordanian people would not stand for it. Nor would the Tartegian people stand for it if the situations were reversed. It must be Martin Bane."

"If your kidnapping is any indication, Bane will honor a contract to the letter," I said. "No more and no less."

Callan was surprised, "Are you saying my kidnapping was contracted? But who would do-?"

She was interrupted by the rasp of steel as Raoul drew his sword.

IN THE NET

I stepped between Raoul and Princess Callan, grabbing his sword arm with both hands. He may have the nickname Spare Prince, but Raoul had received the full martial training a prince would be expected to have. Raoul dropped backward, pulled me off my feet, planted a foot in my chest, and flipped me over him.

I'd had martial training, too. Tucking and rolling, I drew my sword as I came to my feet. But that left Raoul between me and the princess. Unable to risk allowing him to turn away from me, I attacked. Raoul parried and then pressed an attack. Behind Raoul, I saw Tristan pull Callan away from us. At least she was safe for the moment.

Nist caught my attention and signaled toward a point on the deck. Once he was sure I had seen his signal, he ran toward the boom with the net. Of course. If I could draw Raoul to the net, Nist could drop it on us. Steel rang as Raoul blocked all of my thrusts and slashes. Hate blazed up in his eyes and he attacked me with cold fury. I was sure no one who called him the Spare Prince had ever crossed blades with Raoul. There was nothing "spare" about the lethal warrior before me.

Callan was calling for us both to stop fighting. I was willing, but I doubted Raoul would go along with the idea. I fell back again, stepping beneath the net, and smiled as Raoul pressed after me.

"Now, Nist!" I yelled.

The net dropped on top of the two of us. Nist pulled another lever. Raoul and I were thrown off our feet as one edge of the net swept along the deck and under us. Ropes from the boom hoisted the net off the deck. Immediately, Raoul began sawing at the net with his sword.

"Push us over the railing, Nist," I said.

Nist shoved the boom. Raoul froze as we swung over the railing. Fear replaced the hatred in his eyes as the net bobbed and swung, nothing but open space yawning beneath us.

"Tristan, will you take her Highness to her meeting with Martin Bane and safely home once the trogs are defeated?" I asked.

"You have my word," he replied.

"Nist," I said, "release the net."

THE REAL TRAITOR

"No! Don't do it," shouted Raoul.

Nist had never made a move. I had already seen how he and Tristan used the net to frighten potential criminals, so it was what I'd expected of him.

"You can pull them back over the deck, Nist," Tristan ordered.

I added, "But don't release us from the net until Raoul drops his sword."

Nist looked to Tristan, who nodded. Raoul looked to Callan, who nodded, too.

"You will not be harmed," she said. "You have my word."

"Provided he doesn't attack anyone," I amended.

Callan rolled her eyes, "Rob taught you too well."

The pain of Rob's death lingered in Callan's eyes, belying her light tone. But the issue of Raoul required all of her attention now. I could almost see her push the pain aside.

Raoul slid his sword through the net and dropped it to the deck. Nist grabbed it before freeing the two of us from the net. Callan glared at Raoul.

"You drew your sword for no reason. You must have known it would provoke David's reaction. Explain yourself," she demanded.

"May I add a question of my own, Highness?" I asked.

At her nod, I said, "Why were you wining and dining with the captain of that cargo ship?"

"I...was...negotiating with him," Raoul said. Seeing disbelief on my face, he continued, "I was. I offered him a reward if he returned us to Beloren. He's a merchant, not a slaver. All I had to do was make it worth his while to take us back."

"That sounds reasonable to me, David," Callan said. She turned her glare on Raoul again, "Of course, he could have told me what he was doing."

"It does sound reasonable," I conceded. "But on deck, the captain called to his crew in *your* language, Highness, and he does not speak it. I think Raoul taught the captain that sentence during his *negotiations*."

"I did no such thing," protested Raoul.

"I think Raoul had escape plans of his own," I said. "Plans that would make him appear to be dashing and heroic."

"That's the stupidest thing I've ever heard," Raoul sneered.

"How better to throw off the mantel of Spare Prince than to pull off a daring rescue of your future queen? And that's why he drew his sword," I said. "He had to kill me before I revealed just how pathetic he really is."

Raoul responded, "I drew my sword to protect Princess Callan from the real traitor among us. I drew it to protect her from *you!*"

WHO DO YOU BELIEVE?

Raoul's accusation hung in the air. Tristan, Nist, and, worst of all, Callan stared at me. Not one voice was raised in protest.

Sensing he might have an opening for attack, Raoul struck again, "It's obvious that he's working with Bane. Think about it, Callan. They both claim to be one of these Terran Scouts, whatever that means. They both have that Boost thing. Bane understood Rice's weapon *and* used it to save Rice's life when Bane had the upper hand. What kind of raider would risk losing such a powerful weapon merely to save an *enemy*?"

He looked at Callan, "Haven't you wondered why Bane just walked away after you shot the tammar with the Onesie? He knew it couldn't be fired again. Bane could have simply used the Boost to recapture you. He didn't because his *agent* was in place. Rice and Bane have been manipulating events from the beginning."

Raoul turned to me, "Who were you saving Callan from? Why, Bane and his men. It's easy to be the hero when the villain is planning your every move to make you look good. Go ahead, Rice, try to deny it."

I looked at the people around me. Nist was enthralled by the whole story, caught up in the excitement of heroism, villainy, and betrayal. Tristan looked thoughtful, as if considering Raoul's accusations. Callan looked torn between the undeniable logic of Raoul's charges and the emotional bond events had forged between us.

"Of course I deny it," I said. "Though I must say you've given a masterful performance, Raoul-"

"*Prince* Raoul," he said.

"Oh, shut up," I retorted. "I have sworn no oaths to you and owe you no allegiance. And, after *your* action in all of this, I have no respect for you. I will no longer grant you any unearned honorifics."

Ignoring Raoul's sputtering, I continued, "Raoul's words twist events to his benefit, Your Highness. But back on Terra, we have a saying. Actions speak louder than words. You've witnessed my actions and heard Raoul's words. Your Highness, I have a simple question for you."

Capturing Callan's eyes with mine, I asked, "Who do you believe?"

ROB GAVE YOU HIS SWORD

"You must believe me," Raoul said. "I am a prince of Tarteg. My integrity cannot be questioned."

"Sure it can," I said. "And after I question your integrity, I'll question your intelligence."

"You insolent, common dog! I'll-"

"*Be silent!*" Callan demanded.

It never occurred to me to disobey.

"Have any of you heard how Rob became captain of my guard?" Callan asked us.

"I... No," I answered.

"Just before my fourth birthday, there was a conspiracy to kidnap me. Several renegade nobles wished to use me as leverage to force my father to support something or other. I was too young to understand the details and, even now, cannot imagine how they expected to succeed," Callan said.

"Many among the palace guard were bribed, including the captain of the guard. Others cooperated because their families had been threatened. On the chosen night, no guards stood between the kidnappers and my room. Just past midnight, the door to my room burst open, frightening me terribly. I began to cry as my lone defender, a young guard recently assigned to my detail, leapt to defend me.

"That guard was Rob. He placed me into a nook in the room, one designed specifically for such a purpose, and drew his sword. Though there were five kidnappers, no more than two could attack Rob at one time.

As I huddled in the nook, crying, his voice rose over the ring of steel. He told me to stop my crying, that there was nothing to worry about. And then, out-numbered five to one, Rob began to tell me my favorite bedtime story. The familiar cadence of the story and his deep, reassuring voice calmed me as he spoke and his sword sang. One attacker fell. Then another. When the third man dropped, the other two ran.

"Rob sagged onto the floor, holding the worst of his wounds with one hand and cradling me on his lap with the other. Servants and other guards arrived, but he refused to leave my side until my parents were escorted into my room by their own guards. And he finished telling the story."

"A month later, as part of my birthday celebration, Rob was named captain of my guard. My father had his best smiths work around the clock to forge a special sword in honor of Rob's actions that night. As a special birthday treat, I was allowed to present him with the sword.

"In all the years he served me, I never saw him voluntarily part with that sword—until the day he died, when he gave his sword to David.

"*That* action spoke volumes. You ask who I trust, David?"

Callan raised her eyes, brimming with tears, to meet mine.

"Rob gave you his sword. How could I *not* trust you?"

IT WAS YOU

"Callan, you can't be serious," cried Raoul. "Some guard gives his sword to a man you barely know–"

"Rob dedicated his life to my service. He never married nor had children, because those kidnappers used threats against wives and children to suborn some of the guards," Callan said. "He was a mentor, a shoulder to cry on, the one person I could count on to always be there for me. He was like a second father to me. Rob was not just *some guard*!"

"I guess that settles the question of Raoul's intelligence," I said. "Though I still want to question his integrity."

Raoul started sputtering again as Callan said, "Have a care, David. Raoul *is* my future brother-in-law."

"Perhaps," I said, "but I'd like to know what else happened when he was in the captain's cabin."

"I have answered that question," Raoul announced. "I negotiated for our release. Nothing else."

"You didn't teach the captain to say 'Our prize is getting away' in the Mordanian language?"

"Why would I do such a thing?"

"I'll answer that once you've answered my last question."

"I taught the captain nothing," Raoul replied. "Ship's captains have been known to memorize foreign phrases for business purposes."

"Yes, they have. It's a common practice everywhere," I said. "But why would he memorize a line in Mordanian to use when he was talking to his *crew*?"

"You're asking me to explain the actions of a common sailor? I have no idea why the captain would do such a thing," Raoul said. "Callan, this indignity has gone on long enough."

"Princess Callan, do you understand the language spoken by the captain?" I asked.

"No," she said. "I never was very good at learning foreign languages."

"Am I safe in assuming Raoul translated for you on the ship?" I asked.

Callan nodded, turning doubting eyes toward Raoul.

"There's your reason, Raoul," I said. "That line was the perfect cue for your heroic entrance, but it only worked if its intended audience—the princess—could understand it."

Raoul protested, his voice filled with indignation, but I barely heard him. The events of the last few days cascaded through my mind and everything clicked.

"It was you," I said, interrupting Raoul. "Everything that's happened over the last several days—from the raider plot to kidnap the princess to the escape from the slave market to the fight on the merchant airship's deck. It was all staged to let you play the hero and rescue the princess."

Without conscious thought, the tip of my sword flashed, pressing against Raoul's neck.

I said, "*You* hired Martin Bane!"

LENIENCY

The silence stretched as all eyes regarded Raoul. Under the combined weight of those stares, Raoul broke.

"*I* did not hire the raiders," he said.

"Look at me," Callan commanded.

Raoul's eyes rose to meet Callan's.

"I believe you, Raoul," she said. "But I also believe you know who *did* hire them."

Raoul nodded fractionally, "I didn't find out until it was too late to warn you. Your airship was already on its way to Tarteg."

"And would you have warned us if you'd known in time?" Callan pressed.

"I...*think* I would have," Raoul said. As Callan shook her head in disgust, he added, "At least I'm being honest."

"Is that supposed to make it all better?" Callan asked.

"No, Callan-"

"You no longer have leave to use my given name."

"Yes...Your Highness," Raoul said. "It's just... Those Mordanian guards and airmen—it's not my fault they died."

"It's not your fault?" Raoul flinched at her tone. "Pray tell whose fault is it?"

Raoul hung his head but held his silence.

"An honorable man would have ended this whole thing at the trading post. One simple word from you and Bane would have left us behind," Callan said. "Not your fault, Raoul? Why don't you tell that to Rob!"

Turning away, Callan said, "Tristan, may I use your cabin? I would be alone, please."

Tristan showed her to the *Pauline's* cabin.

I said, "Tell us who hired Martin Bane."

Raoul's gaze turned defiant, "No."

"My boy, Raoul has already told us," Tristan said. "Only one person could conceive such a convoluted plan to reinvent the Spare Prince."

I was ashamed my emotions had kept me from realizing it sooner.

"I've known some mama's boys in my time," I said, "but never one so pathetic as you! Nist, would you please bind the Mama's Prince? We can't risk letting him have the run of the ship."

Once Raoul was secured, I asked, "Do you have any idea what we should do with him, Tristan?"

"Before retiring, Her Highness left instructions," Tristan said. "When we get to Beloren, we're to find a Tartegian registered airship and turn him over to them."

"That's more leniency than he deserves," I said.

"Perhaps that's true, lad," Tristan said, "but it's politically astute. It speaks well of Princess Callan's intelligence and training that she chose to do it."

We flew on through the darkness, each of us lost in our own thoughts. I had drifted into sleep when a shout from Nist roused me.

"Master," called Nist, pointing ahead of us. "Look!"

Across the plain, a wide-spread glow danced against the horizon. The city of Beloren was in flames.

BANE, YET AGAIN

Fire climbed into the night, raging across Beloren. Dark shapes moved against the flickering light as thousands of airships fled from the conflagration. The smell of smoke was in the air and, if the wind was just right, the smoke also stung our eyes. An ash floated down onto the deck of the airship. A minute later, another ash followed it.

"The city must have been burning for hours if ash has drifted this far," Tristan observed.

"What could have caused this? Is Beloren at war with someone?" I asked.

"The southern city states wage trade wars all the time, but those rarely involve more than import tariffs," Tristan said. "I haven't heard of anything that would provoke something like this."

"It seems too wide-spread to simply be a building fire that got out of control," I said.

"Master," called Nist. "We've got a ship bearing down on us. A very big one."

"See if you can get above it, Nist, but I don't think we need to run from it." Tristan turned to me, "Do you recognize the airship?"

"No, at least not in this light," I said. "Should I?"

"It's a common configuration for Tartegian naval vessels," Tristan said.

"You think it's Bane?" I asked.

"I would suspect so," Tristan responded.

"There's one easy way to find out," I said, cupping my hands. "*Bane*? Is that you making our pilot nervous?"

"I thought that little ship might be you, Rice. Yours is the only ship approaching the city," came the reply. "Permission to come aboard?"

"Why?" I asked, then remembered Princess Callan's plans to meet with Bane. "Never mind. Permission granted, though for you *only*. The rest of your crew stays on your ship. If any of them attempt to board, we'll kill your employer's only son."

A few seconds passed, then, "I have no idea what you're talking about, Rice."

"Since we both know you're lying, I'd suggest you just drop the act, Bane," I called. "We know the whole story."

"From what I've heard of intrigue in the Tartegian court," Tristan murmured, "I seriously doubt that's true."

Bane called, "Believe whatever makes you happy, Rice. But I agree, only I board."

Bane's airship maneuvered alongside the *Pauline*. I held my sword at Raoul's throat as Bane came aboard. True to his word, his airship moved away once he was aboard.

"Why were you looking for me, Bane?" I asked.

"I'm trying to keep your head from ending up on a pike on what's left of the gates of Beloren," Bane said. "The city government doesn't know your name, yet, but they blame you for the fire."

A GRAND PYRE

"That's the most ridiculous thing I've ever heard," I said. "I just discovered the city was burning a few minutes ago. I couldn't have started the fire even if I'd wanted to—which I didn't."

"I didn't say they accuse you of *setting* the fire," Bane said. "I said they blame you *for* the fire."

"That's equally ridiculous," I protested. "I only spent a few hours inside the city. How can I be to blame?"

"The tunnel rats started fires all over the city in retribution for their fellow rats who died during your rescue of the princess and prince," Bane said. "And for forcing them to kill their tammar."

"Are you telling me that saving people from the tunnel rats is a crime?" I asked.

"You won't find any such law on the books," Bane said, "but the city and the tunnel rats have an unspoken agreement. The rats leave respectable, well-to-do citizens alone, preying on the poor and outcasts teeming throughout the city. The city's population of undesirables is kept in check without endangering anyone important. In return, the city leaves the tunnel rats alone.

"According to the unspoken agreement, the lives of the prince and princess were forfeit when they entered the tunnels on their own," Bane said. "By rescuing them, you broke the peace."

Glaring at Raoul, Bane added, "You also saved me from having to do the same thing."

Turning back to me, Bane said, "The debt I incurred for that is repaid with this warning. Keep clear of Beloren and you should be fine. Now, I'm going to recall my ship and-"

"Please stay a while longer," said Callan as she emerged from the cabin. "I have a proposition to discuss with you.."

Callan strode toward us, her face calm and her eyes hard.

"But first, what became of Rob's body?" Callan asked.

"I'm sorry, Your Highness, I took his body to be properly prepared," Bane said, "but the fire changed everything. It was all I could do to escape the flames with my ship and crew."

Callan turned her gaze toward the city, "An entire city burns in response to Rob's death."

"It's as grand a funeral pyre as any man could ask," Bane said.

Callan watched the burning city for a moment and then nodded. Turning back to Bane, she said, "I have need of a fleet of fighting airships. Will you recruit and command such a fleet for me? If you will, how quickly can you recruit the fleet and how much will it cost?"

"The cost depends entirely on what you wish us to fight," Bane replied.

"Trogs," Callan answered.

"Ah, yes, the trog army did appear to be headed toward the Mordanian border. And the navy is sure to be spread far and wide, searching for the heir to the throne." Bane thought for a moment, "Standard mercenary wages for all ships. I'll need one day to recruit the ships."

"Agreed," Callan said.

"*And*," Bane said, "your father will issue a full pardon for one Martin Bane."

A CONTRACT

"A full pardon?" I demanded. "For *you?*"

"You bring up a good point, Rice," Bane said. "Your Highness, change that to a pardon for me, my crew, and the officers and crews of all of the ships who sign up for this venture. After all, you can't expect men to risk imprisonment or execution at the hands of those they've come to aid."

"I am willing to grant a temporary stay of arrests and prosecution for all officers and crew, but only for the duration of their employment," Callan offered.

"Unacceptable," Bane countered. "Once the Mordanian navy has regrouped and we are deep within Mordan's borders, what keeps you from discharging us from your service and ordering your navy to attack us?"

"You have my word of honor as a princess of the royal house of Mordan."

Bane retorted, "That's very generous of you, I'm sure, but I prefer something tangible. Something in writing that I can show to, say, a naval ship's captain."

"What if my father refuses to honor my pardon?" Callan countered. "He is not bound to honor any agreements I make in his name."

"He may not be legally bound to honor the agreement, but if he doesn't he'll risk casting doubt on all documents signed in his stead by his diplomats," Bane said. "No, Highness, I have full confidence that he'll honor your agreement."

"You know I have little choice and you drive a hard bargain, sir," Callan said. "Very well, I agree to your terms provided we include one final condition. Upon completion of this contract, you leave Mordan and, on pain of death, never cross her borders again."

Bane's eyebrows arched, "Well, Your Highness, that addition was unexpected. Your father will be proud. With reluctance, I accept." Bane flashed a smile. "I suppose this means I'm off the invitation list for the wedding?"

Early morning light bathed the deck before the signing, sealing, and planning was complete.

Returning Bane to his ship, we gave Beloren a wide berth as we steamed north toward the rendezvous point where the fleet would gather. We spotted no Tartegian vessels along the way, leaving us with little choice but to keep the Spare Prince aboard.

Throughout the afternoon and into the night, a motley assortment of airships joined us. At dawn, we counted twenty-one ships flying north behind the *Pauline*.

A tight smile played across Callan's lips. "Let's go hunting."

THUNDER ON HIGH

It took us two days to cross the desert. Bane spent half that time on board *Pauline* planning strategy and tactics with Princess Callan. And, during a break in the planning, I had the chance to speak with Bane.

"You know, Raoul tried to convince Her Highness that I was in league with you," I said.

Bane arched an eyebrow. "Really? How did he do that?"

"He claimed you knew the Onesie was useless after Her Highness shot the tammar and only walked away because your agent—me, according to Raoul—was in place," I explained. "And, much as it pains me to admit it, Raoul has a point. Why did you walk away when you had the upper hand?"

"Yes, I knew the Onesie wasn't a threat. But you were a different matter," Bane responded. "My men had already run away, leaving me to face Rob, a trained warrior, and you, another Scout. Even Boosted, it was a fight I didn't think I could win."

"But I'd already overtaxed my Boost against the trogs."

"I didn't know that," Bane insisted. "Besides, there was only one place you could go if you wanted to survive in the desert. With an airship, I could get to the trading post ahead of you."

I nodded slowly. Bane's explanation made sense.

Finally, our mercenary fleet crossed Mordan's southern border and we began stalking our prey. It was not hard. The trog army had left a trail of devastation a blind man could follow.

Pain and anger warred in Callan's green eyes as we flew over slain people, burned buildings, and tortured land. Tristan, Nist, and I offered comforting words. Even Martin Bane, during our planning sessions offered tentative consolation. Callan would not be consoled, deflecting our words with discussions of tactics.

"We'll be within sight of Faroon within the quarter hour," Callan said, pointing to the horizon. "The city would be a perfect base of operations for the trogs."

"Why?" I asked.

"Faroon is a trading hub," Bane replied. "This time of year, with the harvests recently gathered, the warehouses will be filled with food from all over. The navy keeps a squadron there to patrol the border and deter smuggling. But, like the rest of the navy, they'll probably be searching for the princess. If the trogs have taken Faroon—which seems certain, at this point—we won't be able to force them out of the city."

"You're right," Callan agreed, "but we will control the skies. We'll be able to keep them pinned down in the city while we send airships in search of reinforcements."

Wind whipped around us, making the ship's lines sing, and clouds as dark as our mood scuttled above us. Bane nodded agreement with Callan as the first drops of rain hit the deck. "It will be difficult, Your Highness. The trogs will be free to do what they wish to the city's population. You must prepare yourself to endure it."

"With all the food in the warehouses, won't there be lots of airships docked in the city, as well?" I asked.

"I expect so." Bane said. "What of it?"

"Well, what if the trogs have captured merchant airships?" I asked. "Couldn't they mount an aerial defense of the city?"

"No," Bane said. "Trogs don't use airships."

An unbroken rumble of thunder sounded above us.

"Yes, but trogs don't form armies, either," I said.

Bane looked at me in surprise then turned to look up at the clouds.

"What do you-" I began.

"Quiet," Bane ordered. A few seconds later, he cried, "That sound isn't thunder."

Bane ran back to his own ship, shouting orders. "Emergency signal to the fleet. There are enemy ships above us!"

Lightning flashed and real thunder roared as airships filled with trogs dropped out of the clouds.

TROGS ON DECK

As the airships drew nearer, it became clear that the trogs were not flying them. Men handled the airships, though they did not do so willingly. People—men, women, even children—were tied to railings, hostages to force the cooperation of those flying the ships.

Bane called across to me, "Rice, get away from the battle. You're not a warship and your crew is too small to repel boarders for very long. Besides, we can't risk losing our employer."

"You're all heart, Bane," I called back, but he had already turned his attention back to the coming battle.

Nist had heard Bane's instructions and was already steering away from the fight. I ran to Callan's side.

"We've got to free Raoul," I said. "We may need his sword if trogs try to board us."

"I'll go get him," she said, then added, "He's much more likely to listen to me than you."

The air battle began taking shape behind us. The trog airships outnumbered us, but our crews had their hearts and minds focused on the fight. The enemy airships were sluggish, as the trogs could only pass orders by pointing. Our ships maneuvered crisply as experienced crews sprang to obey orders from the ship's officers. The situation was dire, but victory *was* possible.

Nist shouted to catch my attention, then pointed back through the rain. Two trog ships had broken off from the main battle and were following us. We couldn't outrun them because we didn't have a full head of steam built up. We hadn't been expecting trouble—famous last words—so weren't able to simply fly away from the larger ships.

Nist spun the wheel and worked the ailerons with frantic intensity, bobbing and weaving, working to keep the trog airships from boxing us in. During one close swing by one of the airships, I saw one of the trogs plunge a spear into one of the hostages, all the while shouting at the crew.

Callan and Raoul stumbled out of the cabin, both of them clutching swords.

"David, what is Nist doing?" Callan called, trying to keep her balance. Then she spotted the trog airships and no longer needed an answer.

The trogs must have realized the *Pauline* was too agile and Nist too skillful for their airships to cut us off. The trogs began throwing things at Nist. Boathooks, belaying pins, anything solid they could lay their hands on rained down on the *Pauline*. It didn't take very long for something to hit him. Nist collapsed as a boathook smashed into his head. Without Nist working the controls, the *Pauline's* flight path straightened out.

I rushed to take the wheel but it was too late. With a thud, the first trog landed on the deck.

TAKE THE WHEEL

The airship rocked under the trog and he fought for balance. I kicked him in the chest. He stumbled backward and toppled over the railing. Raoul thrust his sword through the next trog to land on the deck. Two more trogs jumped down as Raoul pulled his blade free of the dead trog. I slashed wildly at each, driving both back a couple of steps, but three more of them jumped onto our airship.

"Princess," I called, "take the wheel. Steer as wildly as you can. It should keep the trogs off balance and make it harder for more of them to jump to the deck."

Raoul ducked under a spear thrust, cutting the trog's legs out from under him.

"Raoul, come over here," I called. "We need to fight back to back and defend the princess."

Callan took the wheel and spun it hard. The deck reeled beneath our feet. Raoul stumbled toward me and I caught him. We each grabbed hold of a ship's line with our free hand, using it as an anchor against the wild swings of the deck. Three trogs mistimed their jumps, plunging past the ship as the four remaining trogs lumbered toward us.

"I thought you were some kind of super swordsman, Rice," Raoul said. "Use your boost thing."

I drove my sword at a trog's face and he dove to the deck.

"I won't use the Boost unless the situation gets really bad," I said.

Raoul swung on his line, kicking a trog in the face.

"This isn't really bad?" Raoul asked. "How can it get much worse, man?"

The sound of ripping fabric came from above, answering Raoul's question. A trog had hit the airship's envelope rather than its deck. Trying to steady himself with his spear, the trog had torn a long gash in the airship's envelope. The unpredictable gyrations had thrown the trog off, but the damage had been done.

Hot air gushed through the gash and the *Pauline* lost altitude rapidly. I hazarded a look below. Our flight had taken us over the city of Faroon.

We were going down into a city full of trogs.

DOWNED IN THE CITY OF THE TROGS

I wrenched my attention back to the deck of the *Pauline*. Two of the remaining trogs had caught their balance and were advancing on Raoul and me. With Boost I could take all five trogs by myself, but the city was bound to be far more dangerous than this. I had no choice but to save my Boost. At least the two trog airships had returned to the aerial battle once it was obvious we were going down inside the city.

I dodged a trog spear thrust then sliced open the trog's arm with my counter. He dropped his spear and fell back, howling. Turning to face the other way, I ducked under Raoul's defense and thrust my blade through the chest of the trog he'd been fighting.

Leaving my sword in the dying trog, I charged the unwounded trog. His footing still unsure on the rolling deck, the trog managed to regain his balance just as I barreled into him. Legs churning, I drove him backward and over the railing.

As I returned to retrieve my sword, Raoul cut the throat of the last unwounded trog. The remaining trog, blood dripping from his wounded arm, jumped from the airship as we passed over a tall building.

Callan searched for a place to land the airship while Tristan tended to Nist. Running to the bow, I scanned the city for a defensible place to land.

"Callan," I said, pointing, "there's a walled garden over there. Can you land inside the walls?"

"I can try," she replied.

"But I can do it," Nist said, "if someone can help me stand at the controls."

Tristan easily lifted the smaller man and braced him at the wheel. Callan came to my side as Nist worked the ship's wheel and ailerons. Just when I thought Nist had overshot the garden, he twisted the ailerons. The little ship nosed up then dropped into the garden.

Guttural trog shouts came from streets all around us. We were stranded in the city of the trogs.

THE ALLEY

The *Pauline's* deflating envelope was still floating above the garden wall, visible to every trog in the area. We had bare minutes before the trogs found us. As much as I hated to leave it, we couldn't hide with the airship. Parts of its superstructure rose above the garden wall. Even after the envelope deflated, the ship would be easy to spot.

"Everybody out and into the house," I said. "We've got to find some sort of defensible location before the trogs find us."

The house wasn't what we needed—it was too close to the airship—but it was all we had at the moment. I'd see what we had to work with inside and then take it from there.

The calls of trogs sounded much closer as we ran into the house. Someone—probably the trogs—had been here first. Smashed furniture lay all around, dashing any hope of using the furniture as a barricade. The ground floor was too open for our small number, anyway.

"Upstairs," Raoul said, heading for the stairs.

"No," I countered, "we'd be trapped up there. The trogs could just starve us out or decide to burn the house down around us. We have to find another place to hole up."

I looked out the windows on the front of the house. The street before us was clear for the moment.

"Does everyone see that alley over there?" I asked, pointing out the window. "That's where we're heading. Raoul, take point. I'll take rear guard. Raoul, if you find a place to hide, do *not* wait for me. Go to ground and keep the princess safe."

"Leaving you to die at the hands of the trogs?" asked Raoul. "I can live with that."

"No, David," Princess Callan said, "we'll get out of this together or we won't get out at all."

"We don't have time for a debate, Highness," I said. "Please shut up and let me do the job I swore to do."

Callan's cheeks reddened—whether in anger or embarrassment, I couldn't tell—but she nodded. Then we ran for the alley.

We were halfway to the alley when five trogs rounded a corner and spotted us. The trogs began yelling and gave chase. We ran into the alley, finding it clear. Our hope for escape only lasted for a few seconds. Another trog patrol entered the far end of the alley. Behind us, the first patrol blocked the other end of the alley.

We were trapped.

RAOUL RUNS

S houting and waving their spears, the trogs bore down on us from both ends of the alley. I looked for doors but found none opening into the alley except on the other side of the trogs. The only way out of the alley was to go through the trogs—or *over* them.

"Callan," I said. "can you climb to the roof?"

Before she could answer, a rope dropped in front of her.

"Climb the rope!" a boy's voice called. "Hurry!"

The trogs would reach us before everyone could climb to the roof, but with some teamwork, most of us could get away. I charged the trogs on my end of the alley, calling over my shoulder, "Raoul, hold off the other trogs while the rest climb the rope."

Grabbing the rope, Raoul sneered. "I do not die so commoners can survive. It is the place of commoners to die so I can survive."

I slashed at the leading trogs, slowing their charge, then ran back to the princess. I'd have to stay close to her so I could guard her from both groups of trogs.

"Climb, Highness," I said.

"No, David," she said. "I can fight. Just give me-"

"Dammit, Callan, if I'm going to die, let it be protecting *you*, not your corpse," I said, shoving the rope into her hands.

Callan's face fell and, without another word, she began pulling herself up the rope.

Nist held the rope out to Tristan, "You're next, Master."

"No, Nist, I'm too old, too fat, and too slow. I'll get us both killed if I go next."

I never heard Nist's reply.

Boost!

I rolled under the closest trog's spear, gutting him as I came to my feet. I charged into the trogs behind the one I'd just killed. Dodging, spinning, slashing, and thrusting, I drove the first squad of trogs away from the rope.

With these trogs on their heels, I rushed at the other squad. I passed Nist, who stood white-faced, guarding the rope as Tristan labored to climb it. On the roof, Callan and the boy heaved on the rope, trying to speed Tristan's ascent.

At least Callan was safely on the roof. Raoul was nowhere to be seen. I'd be lying if I said I was surprised.

The trogs before me lowered their spears, as if expecting me to attack from below as I had with the first squad. Instead, I leapt up and pushed off the wall, surprising the trogs. Their spears tangled as they tried to raise them. Taking that opening, I barreled into them, slicing a throat, slashing a shoulder, piercing an eye, forcing them to fall back.

Once again, I broke away from the squad I was fighting and ran back toward the rope. Nist was scampering up the rope just out of reach of the regrouped first squad. One trog drew his spear back, preparing to throw it at Nist. I drove into the trog at a full run, running him through before he could impale Nist.

"David," Callan called, "Climb the rope."

It was too late. Both squads of trogs had reached the rope. Spears jabbing, the trogs backed me against the far wall. I was cut off from the rope.

KEEPING TROGS AT BAY

Spear points bristled around me, jabbing and thrusting. I dodged and ducked, slashing and stabbing, keeping the trogs at bay. Even facing the unimaginative trog attacks, I knew I had little time remaining. I'd dodge when I should have ducked or, if I was lucky, hang on long enough to suffer Boost burnout, but the trogs would get me in the end. It would be worth it as long as Callan was getting away.

She wasn't, of course. Several people moved on the roof opposite me, manhandling something to the edge of the roof.

"David," she called, "we found a rain barrel. Be ready to climb the rope."

They shoved the barrel over the roof edge and it dropped on the trogs. Two trogs fell when, with a crack, the barrel burst on top of them. Water gushed, washing aside the trogs at the bottom of the rope. My path to the roof was clear. I leapt across the alley and pulled myself up the rope. A spear clattered against the wall as I rolled onto the roof. The boy yanked the rope up behind me as Nist dragged me away from the edge of the roof.

Safe for the moment, I released Boost—and didn't black out. It was a pleasant change of pace. The fight must have been shorter than I had realized. Or maybe I was adjusting to the Boost.

That was a point for the techs to figure out, if they ever found a safe way to reach me.

Nist helped me to my feet and we moved away from the alley full of frustrated trogs.

"I don't suppose Raoul is off scouting for a hiding place?" I asked.

"Is he the jerk who came up the rope first?" the boy asked.

Astute lad. I liked him already.

"Yes," I said. "And thank you for your help. We would have been captured or killed without it."

The boy smiled, "Teach me how to fight like you do and we'll call it even."

"We'll talk about that later," I said. "Do you have a safe place to hide?"

"Yeah," he said, heading across the roof. "Come on."

There were so many twists, turns, ascents, and descents that I was completely disoriented by the time the boy led us into a small cellar. In the corner, a pale young woman lay huddled on a small bed.

"I need your help finding a doctor," the boy said. "I think my sister is dying."

THE DESERT DOCTOR

Tristan crossed to the bed, knelt beside it, and pulled back the blanket covering the young woman. He grimaced as he examined the deep wound in her side.

"Nist, I'm going to need my medical kit and supplies," he said. "Boiling water would be useful, too."

"Your supplies are on the *Pauline*, master," Nist said.

"The boy should be able to lead you back to the airship," Tristan said. "You'd do that wouldn't you, boy?"

"My name is Milo," the boy said, "and I'll do anything to help Kim."

Callan knelt next to Tristan, asking, "You're a physician?"

"I am."

"You never told us that," I said.

"My life has been rather busy since you dropped into it, lad," Tristan said. "Besides, you never asked. Would you please go with Nist and Milo and keep them safe."

"Highness, may I have your permission to accompany them?" I asked.

"Of course, David," Callan said.

Nist described the house where he had landed the *Pauline*.

Milo nodded, "I know where that is."

Once we were back on the rooftops, Milo asked, "Is that woman really a princess?"

"So they tell me—and I have no reason to doubt their word," Nist answered. "She is Princess Callan, daughter of your king. This is David Rice, her royal bodyguard."

"Yeah?" Milo said, looking at me. "I'd take your job in a heart-beat. I'd guard her royal body real close, if you know what I mean."

Based on his size, I'd originally estimated Milo's age to be ten. After this revelation, I revised it up to thirteen or fourteen. He must be quite small for his age.

Nist tried hard to smother a laugh, not succeeding particularly well, "Her Highness is quite beautiful."

Milo pointed across a several rooftops, "Is that the house where you landed." Nist nodded and Milo continued, "If we get these supplies, do you think Kim will be okay? Is the old guy a good doctor?"

"His skills are legend among the tribes of the desert," Nist replied.

Milo spun around, "He's the guy they call the Desert Doctor?"

"That he is," Nist replied. "Your sister is in excellent hands."

We moved parallel to a wide street, waiting to get as close to the house as possible before dropping to street level. Then I heard trog voices from the street below.

"Quiet!" I hissed, pulling Milo and Nist to their knees.

I crawled to the roof edge and looked down at the road. A squad of trogs prodded a man with their spears. The man's hands were tied behind his back and he faced away from me, but I'd have recognized him anywhere.

The trogs had captured Prince Raoul.

RESCUING RAOUL

Raoul jumped as a trog poked his backside with a spear. The other trogs wheezed. Laughter, I assumed. Another poke, another jump, more wheezing.

"The jerk got caught," Milo whispered. "Serves him right for running off."

"I should just leave him to his fate," I sighed. "It's what he would do to me."

"But you're not going to leave him," Milo said. "Because you're not like him."

"No, I'm not going to leave him," I said. "Rescuing Raoul should draw trog patrols this way. You two, get the medical kit then go straight back to the hiding place. Don't wait for me. I can find my way back there, I think."

"The Spare Prince doesn't deserve this," Nist said.

"I'm not doing this for him. I wouldn't be worthy to wear this sword if I just walked away," I said. "Get going."

Bent low, the two ran off. I stalked the trogs from above, waiting until Nist and Milo were long out of sight.

I jumped at the squad below. My slashing blade decapitated the rearmost trog. His head bounced off the street as I tucked and rolled with the landing. I ran another through as I rose to my feet in the middle of the squad. Whipping the blade around, I stabbed into the gut of a trog behind me. That was enough for the two remaining trogs. They ran, leaving Raoul standing above three trog corpses.

"*You!*" Raoul spat, his hatred of me battling across his face with his relief at being rescued.

I guess Raoul wasn't very happy to see me. His hatred won. Raoul's face turned red and he gave into his rage. Hands still tied behind his back, Raoul lowered his head and charged. I was really tired of dealing with Raoul. Stepping into his charge, I put all of my strength and weight behind a right cross. The pommel of my sword smashed into Raoul's temple and he collapsed at my feet. It wasn't very sporting to hit a man whose hands were tied, but it was *very* satisfying.

Cutting off a piece of a dead trog's loincloth, I stuffed it in Raoul's mouth, gagging him. Shouldering Raoul, I found stairs to the rooftops in a nearby alley. Twenty minutes later, I lugged Raoul into the hiding place.

Callan's and Tristan's eyes widened when they recognized Raoul, but I had other worries.

Nist and Milo weren't back.

ROOFTOP CONFRONTATION

"W here are the other two?" Tristan asked.

"We had to split up," I said, dropping Raoul in a corner. "I thought my rescue of the Spare Prince would draw any trog patrols, leaving Nist and Milo clear to go after the medical kit."

"The trogs did that to Raoul?" Callan asked, eying the lump on the side of Raoul's head.

"No, I did."

Callan's left eyebrow arched, so I added, "Raoul took exception to being rescued by me and tried to attack. So, I smacked him on the head."

"Hard?" she asked.

"Very."

"Good," she said. "And now you're going back out to find Nist and Milo?"

"That's the plan."

Callan rose on her toes and kissed me lightly on the lips. "Be careful."

"As you wish, Highness" I said. "Do you mind tying Raoul before he wakes up?"

Callan was happily pulling knots tight around Raoul's wrists as

I left. Soon, I was up on the rooftops, running back the way I had come. Trog shouts and calls echoed through the city, but none of them were anywhere near me. Had the trogs been frightened off by their losses in this area or were they stalking the area in silence? Whatever the reason, the silence allowed other sounds to carry. That's how I heard Milo's voice.

"Give that back," Milo cried. "It's not yours!"

A rough voice answered, "Anything I can take is mine, kid. This bag of medicine will be worth a fortune."

"No. I need it for my sister. She might die without it."

"Sister, eh?" said the voice. "Tell you what, boy, take us to her. I'm sure we'd all like to meet her. And if we like what we see, maybe we'll give her some medicine. I wouldn't want to lose my new plaything too quickly."

Coarse laughter rose from several throats.

"Leave the boy alone," Nist said. "You wanted the medicine and you have it. Take it and go."

I came over a rooftop and saw them on the next roof. Four men surrounded Milo and Nist. Nist stood between Milo and the man holding the medicine kit. Nist also held one hand to his head as blood seeped between his fingers.

"I'm getting tired of his lip," the rough-voiced man said to his men. "Kill him."

BETTER CONNECTIONS

There was no way I could reach Nist before the gang killed him, but there was also no way I was going to let Nist die.

"Kill him," I called, running down the roof, "and you'll answer to me."

My arrival surprised the gang. Seeing me charge down on them, sword drawn, gave rough-voice's men pause. They turned to their leader for instructions.

Rough-voice motioned to the biggest and strongest of the bunch, "Sarn, teach that guy what happens to people who get in my way."

Sarn grinned and charged. The others grinned, too. I guessed Sarn was known for beating down anyone who displeased rough-voice. At least all of the attention was on me and no one was trying to kill Nist.

The way Sarn moved revealed everything to me. He showed no subtlety, no grace. He relied entirely on size and strength. Sarn was a brawler, not a fighter. I wouldn't need Boost to handle him.

As we drew together, I tucked, rolled, and came up at him with my fists together, driving with my legs. Sarn folded around my punch, his breath whooshing out. I flowed into a spin kick and

Sarn reeled. He collapsed, gasping to draw breath, at rough-voice's feet. My sword was at rough-voice's throat before the others could react.

"Let. Them. Go."

The two thugs released Nist and Milo.

"Now the medicine kit," I said to rough-voice. His face darkened, so I added, "You can give it to me or I'll take it from your corpse. It's all the same to me."

"Don't think you've won," rough-voice said, tossing the medicine kit to Nist. "Once the trogs are run out of the city, I'll report you to the authorities. I've got connections in the guard. Who do you think they'll believe, us four citizens or some street urchin and two foreigners?"

The threat was so ludicrous I couldn't help it. I burst out laughing.

"Please do make that report. I'm willing to bet my connections are a tad bit better than yours," I said. Rough-voice's face went slack, unsure how to respond to my laughter. "You deserve a sound thrashing, but I've got more important things to do right now. If I see you again, though..."

I whacked rough-voice on the side of the head with the flat of my blade. He flinched, backed away, then turned and stalked away.

Moments later we were back at Milo's hiding place. Callan drew Milo away from his sister and, with a little prompting, got Milo to launch into a breathless and mostly accurate account of their exploits. Nist gave the kit to Tristan and we joined him at the wounded woman's bedside.

"I've asked Her Highness to keep the boy distracted," Tristan murmured. "His sister has a deep spear wound in her side. The surgery will be tricky and she might not survive it."

SUPPLY SEARCH

I looked at Milo, somersaulting to demonstrate my attack on Sarn. Callan smiled, laughed, and gasped in all the right places, her attention seemingly riveted on Milo. Her eyes betrayed her true emotions—worry for her people, concern for Milo's sister, and sympathy for the boy capering before her.

Milo came to the breathless end of his story, adding, "Now that we've got the medicine, the Desert Doctor will save Kim."

"Such faith the young man has in an old man like me," sighed Tristan.

"He should have faith," said Nist. "But you are not an old man."

"I'm not?" Tristan raised an eyebrow.

"Not at all, Master. You are a *very* old man."

Tristan's lips twitched upward, "That's the final insult I take from you, scamp. I'm writing you out of my will."

Tristan turned to me, "I hate to send you out again, lad, but I need a few medical items for the girl's recovery. I've made a list."

"I can speak this language, Tristan. I can't read it," I said.

"Not surprising, considering how you learned the language. Take Milo. He shouldn't be here during the surgery,

138

anyway," Tristan said. "And remind me to start teaching you to read when we find time to spare."

Milo scanned the list, relieved to have something to do other than sit around and worry about his sister.

"What do you need liquor for?" he asked.

"I don't have any anesthesia in the medicine kit. Drinking it will help Kim with the pain," Tristan said.

"It's not to calm your nerves? My Uncle Torm always said that, but I knew better," Milo said, looking hard at Tristan.

"It most certainly is not," Tristan replied in indignation.

Milo stared at Tristan for another moment. Whatever he saw satisfied him and we headed out. Our first stop was a nearby apothecary. It had already been picked clean.

"Gort and his gang probably took it all," Milo mused.

"Gort's the thug from the rooftop?" At Milo's nod, I continued, "Any idea where we can find him?"

"He'll be holed up in a bar somewhere," Milo said. "I think I know where to look. And liquor is on the list."

Milo led me across the rooftops for nearly a kilometer. It was dusk when he pointed to a bar across the street. I was about to drop to the street when I saw Sarn. He sprinted from an alley, crossed the street, and ran into the bar. That's when we found out we weren't the only ones who had spotted Sarn.

A dozen trogs ran out of the same alley and charged toward the bar.

TROGS AND THUGS

As if my day hadn't been busy enough already, now I was about to risk my life for Gort and his gang of thugs. Well, for their hoard of supplies, anyway. But rescuing the thugs would be a byproduct.

"Milo, stay here and stay hidden," I said. "If I'm not out in fifteen minutes, go report this to the princess."

"Report? That's it?" Milo asked.

"That will be enough. The princess must be told what has happened," I said. Callan would need to be told, but I also didn't want Milo getting himself killed trying to help me. "Can I count on you?"

Milo nodded as shouts rose from the bar. I cast a smile at Milo, jumped down, then dashed across the street and into the bar.

The fading daylight offered little illumination within the bar. Windows on the far side of the room silhouetted the chaos inside. Brawny Sarn swung two big clubs with enough force and wild abandon to keep four trogs at bay. Gort was behind the bar, cocking a crossbow, while the other two thugs stood on the other side of the bar swinging swords with great enthusiasm and little skill. The trogs before them had no more concept of unit tactics than any other trogs I'd fought, allowing the thugs' efforts to be more successful than they deserved to be. One trog lay within the door, a crossbow bolt through one eye.

I couldn't risk Boosting so soon after the fight in the alley. So, instead of charging into the center of the action, I stayed on the outskirts of the fight. A trog lurched back to avoid Sarn's wind-milling clubs. I ran him through before he even knew I was there. Gort fired his crossbow at the same time, the quarrel punching through another trog's chest and out the back. In the confusion caused by the sudden loss of two of their squad, I charged in among the trogs and slashed deeply into another trog's leg. Gort's eyes went wide when he saw me. The wounded trog's leg buckled and he yelled a warning to the others as he fell. Two trogs turned and came at me in a rush, driving me back toward the door.

One of the trogs looked past me to the doorway. Guessing that couldn't be good for me, I jumped to the left. The trog spear meant for my neck gouged my right shoulder. Pain flared from the deep cut and my hand spasmed. With a clatter, my sword fell to the floor, leaving me unarmed and surrounded by trogs.

Spears raised, the trogs closed in for the kill.

I NEED A DOCTOR

With no weapon in hand, I was in big trouble. My only choice was to Boost and hope I'd stay conscious after the fight. I tried not to think how badly things would go for me if Gort and his crew had me at their mercy. Then I heard a *thunk* from behind me. Glancing over my shoulder, I saw the trog in the doorway topple toward me. I spun behind the falling trog, holding him between me and the two other trogs' attacks. The trogs realized their error too late. Two spears plunged into the chest of the trog I held..

Agony shot through my wounded shoulder as I shoved the bleeding trog into the other two. All three went down in a heap. Picking up my sword, I ordered my implant to release a pain killer and a fast-acting analgesic flowed into my blood stream. Agony receding, I finished off the three trogs then rejoined the battle.

A minute later, all of the trogs were dead. One of Gort's sword-wielding thugs was dead and Sarn sat against the back wall holding a deep leg wound. Milo stood at the door, a long, stout piece of wood in his hands.

"I told you to stay on the roof," I said.

"I saw another trog coming to the bar," Milo said. "Kim needs the medicine more than your princess needs a report. Besides, I saved your life."

"Those are all good points," I admitted.

"Ain't that sweet," Gort said. "Now, get out of my bar before I shoot you."

"You're welcome," I said.

Gort stared at me.

"For saving your worthless lives," I said.

"We didn't need none of your help," he said.

"Are you delusional?" I asked. "I killed six of the trogs and my friend took care of a seventh. You'd be dead or captured without us."

"Gort?" said Sarn. "I need a doctor."

Gort said, "We don't got a doctor."

"I do," I said. "The Desert Doctor is part of my group. I'll take Sarn to him in exchange for the supplies I need."

Gort shook his head, "Sorry Sarn, that cut ain't worth giving away any of my supplies. Time to prove how tough-"

A chair smashed over Gort's head. His eyes rolled back in his head and he crumpled to the floor.

"You really got a doctor?" the third thug asked.

"Yes," I said.

"You and the kid carry the supplies," he said. "I'll help Sarn."

Minutes later, Tal—the third thug—braced Sarn and we headed out into a city teeming with trogs. We were in no condition for any kind of fight. Darkness and luck were our only allies. I prayed they would be enough for us to get back to Milo's hiding place.

THE ANSWER

We moved at a snail's pace. Crossing the street seemed to take forever, but it was fast compared to the climb to the rooftops. Unable to run for cover, we froze at every sound. The thirty minute trip to the bar dragged out to a two and a half hour trek back. Sarn was exhausted from blood loss and pain and the rest of us were all on edge by the time we got to the hiding place.

One look at Callan showed that I'd had the far easier task. She sat huddled in a corner, hugging her knees, her face drawn and pale. She was absently twiddling a thick leather strap. It was damp with saliva and had fresh bite marks ground into it. Without anesthesia for Milo's sister, the surgery must have been horribly painful for Kim and horribly unnerving for Callan.

Tristan took charge of the medical supplies, ordering Nist to prepare various concoctions for Kim's wound. While Nist was busy with the medicine, Tristan examined Sarn's wound and mine. Proclaiming mine to be a minor wound and not in need of immediate attention, Tristan selected a bottle of liquor. With a nod toward Callan, he gave it to me.

I crossed to where Callan sat and, sinking to the floor, offered the bottle to Callan, "Drink."

She didn't take the bottle, but her eyes widened when she saw my bloody shoulder.

"Tristan says it's not serious," I said, pressing the bottle to her lips and tilting it up. "Now, drink."

Callan swallowed. Her cheeks flushed and her eyes watered.

"Are you trying to poison me, David?" she gasped.

"Doctor's orders," I said, waving the bottle toward Tristan before also taking a drink. "Now, tell me about it or I'll give you another drink."

Callan leaned into me and I drew her close. From his corner, the trussed-up and now-conscious Raoul glared at me.

Callan looked at Milo's sister. "She was so brave during the surgery. She never cried out once, but she nearly bit through the leather strap."

Once Callan began, the words tumbled out. Callan told me of the pain reflected in Kim's eyes as Tristan operated, her crushing grip as Callan held her hand, her unending stream of tears, and how she held her body rigidly still so Tristan could operate.

"I felt so helpless," Callan said. "All I could do was stroke her head, hold her hand, offer empty words, and look her in the eye."

I wrapped my other arm around her, holding her tightly. Before I could offer my own empty words, Tal squatted down before me.

"The doctor said I should talk to you," he said. "He says maybe I got the answer."

"The answer to what?" I asked.

Tal replied, "Beating the trogs."

BEATING THE TROGS

"You know how to get rid of the trogs?" I asked.

Tal said, "The doctor says I do."

"Well?"

Tal's brow furrowed. It was easy to see how Tal had fallen in with Gort. Tal was a born follower, not particularly bright and generally happy to have someone else making his decisions for him. It made his attack against Gort all the more surprising. Sarn must be a really good friend for Tal to have taken such initiative.

"What did you say before the doctor sent you to me?' I asked.

Tal's face cleared, "I was talking to him about the challenges."

"What challenges?"

"The big trog has one every morning," Tal said. "At dawn, an old guy with the trog calls for a challenger."

"Guy? You mean a man?"

"Yeah, he's a man but he talks trog, too," Tal said.

"Tell me about the challenge," I said.

"Not much to tell," he replied. "Sometimes a prisoner volunteers, sometimes the trogs pull a prisoner out of the crowd. They fight, the man dies, and then the trogs all chant something."

"Is there anything else you can remember?" I asked.

Tal shook his head but Milo, who had been listening from his sister's bedside, nodded.

"Yeah, there's one more thing," Milo said. "When the trogs pull a challenger out of the pen, they just toss the body on a big fire when the fight is over. When someone volunteers to fight the leader, the trogs make a pyre and hold a short ceremony. It's like a trog funeral or something."

That was interesting and might even give some insight into trog culture.

"Do they fight with weapons or is it hand-to-hand?" I asked.

"People who volunteer get to choose weapons," Milo said. "The ones they pull from the pen have to fight hand-to-hand."

"Thank you, both. That's very helpful," I said.

Tal went back to Sarn and Milo turned his attention back to his sister.

"A lot of primitive cultures allow challenges to determine tribal supremacy," I said. "Holding a challenge each morning is a simple way for the leader to demonstrate his dominance over the humans in the city."

"You don't know if that's what the trog leader is doing," Callan said.

"It makes sense, Callan," I said. "Warrior cultures respect courage, so the bodies of those who volunteer to fight are treated with respect."

From the other corner, Raoul rocked back and forth, trying to talk around the gag I'd stuffed in his mouth.

"Tal," I said, "take the gag out of his mouth."

Tal did and Raoul spat, "There's no need to risk your precious royal guard, Callan. I will challenge the trog leader."

REQUEST AND REQUIRE

et Raoul challenge the trog leader. That was such a tempting thought that I almost agreed to it. But no matter the appeal of the idea, it was one fraught with problems of its own.

"It has to be me," I said to Callan. "You can't allow Raoul to go in my place.

"How very noble of you," Raoul sneered. "This is your chance to save your lover, Callan. You can always send him off to be killed if I fail."

"Tal?" I asked. "Put the gag back in the prince's mouth."

"I forbid that, peasant," Raoul snarled.

Tal backed away, saying, "I don't think so. He might bite me."

"He's just desperate enough that he might," I agreed. "If he does, you have my permission to hit his head against the wall until he stops biting."

Tal brightened, "Thanks."

"You cretin!" Raoul said. "I'll see you hanged for-"

Tal stuffed the gag in Raoul's mouth, cutting him off. Raoul did not bite Tal. I was a little disappointed. I think I would have enjoyed watching Raoul's head bounce off the wall a few times.

"You keep insisting I shouldn't send Raoul. Why?" Callan asked.

"I think you know the reasons, Highness," I said. "First, he could run off. I know that's not very heroic, but Raoul isn't much of a hero."

That earned Raoul's nastiest glare yet.

"He could lose the challenge," I continued, "leaving you to explain to his family—including your future husband—why you allowed a Tartegian prince to die fighting Mordan's battle. And if Raoul won, you'd have to explain to the Mordanian people why a Tartegian prince fought to save them while a Mordanian guardsman stood by."

"Oh, David," Callan said, "losing Rob has been hard enough. I don't think I could bear it if I lost you, too."

"You're stronger than you think Callan. You can bear it," I said. "You *will* bear it if necessary. Your people need you to be strong enough to do that which must be done."

Callan sighed and pulled away from me. She composed herself and the tired, frightened young woman was replaced by the regal Princess Callan, heir to the throne of Mordan.

In formal tones, she said, "David Rice, Captain of my Royal Guard, I request and require you to save my people. At dawn, you will challenge the trog leader and defeat him in single combat."

ACCEPT AND ACCEDE

"**R**equeshed and require?" a voice slurred before I could answer. "Ish she some kinda prinshesh or shomething?"

"Kim," cried Milo, a grin splitting his face. "You're alive! And awake. And drunk."

Milo rushed to his sister, quickly followed by Tristan and Nist. Sarn and Tal appeared to have fallen asleep against the far wall. Only Raoul saw Callan take me by the hand and pull me outside.

She led me up to the rooftop and then melted against me. We just held each other and it was as if time no longer existed. All our worries faded into the background as we lived in the moment.

"David? Your Highness?" Milo's voice broke the spell. He came up onto the rooftop and saw us. "Whoa! Hey, sorry. I didn't mean to interrupt."

"What is it, Milo?" Callan asked, looking his way but staying wrapped in my arms.

"Tristan and I just wanted to make sure you two were safe," Milo said. Ducking back toward the hiding place, he added, "I'm glad you're taking your job seriously, David."

Callan cast a quizzical look at me, "What does that mean?"

"I'm, um, guarding your royal body," I grinned.

Callan clapped a hand over her mouth to stifle a giggle and her body shook as she laughed for the first time in days. It was good to hear her laugh. And it was good to feel her laughter, too.

When she was still again, I said, "I don't know the formal words to answer your question."

"I know your answer, David," Callan said. "But the formal phrase is *accept and accede*."

"What is it with royalty and alliteration?" I asked. "Request and require, accept and-"

Callan pulled my head down toward hers. "Oh hush and kiss me."

"I accept and accede," I replied.

Then time went away again.

Callan and I were dozing in each other's arms when Tristan and Tal came for me.

"It'll be dawn soon," Tristan said. "Time to go, lad."

Tal, my guide, was armed with a crossbow and a sword.

I gave Callan a last embrace then shook Tristan's hand. For his ears only, I said, "If anything happens to me, Tristan..."

"I'll see her safely home, lad," he said. "You can count on that."

I shared one last look with Callan, then Tal and I set off to challenge the trog leader.

CHALLENGING THE GREAT ONE

We made our way across the rooftops in silence. Only as we neared the center of town did Tal break the silence.

"This is gonna be easy for you, right?"

"Why do you think that?" I asked.

"Because you can do that boost thing. The kid, Milo, he told me about it," Tal replied.

"It's not as useful against a single opponent as you might think," I said. "A group never has the time to adjust to my quickness and that messes up their teamwork. Many times they end up hurting themselves more than I hurt them. A single fighter can adjust faster and better."

"If you say so," Tal muttered, unconvinced.

"I'll use it if things get really desperate," I added, "But I'd rather save the Boost in case I have to make a run for it after the fight. Like if the trogs attack me if I win."

Tal nodded, that last bit seemed to make sense to him.

By that time we had reached the rooftops overlooking the trog camp. It sprawled throughout the town square and into a small park next to the square. The sky was just bright enough for me to make out a few details. Trogs were everywhere; cooking, eating, sharpening spears, standing guard, or just sitting around doing nothing. On the edge of the park, a rough fence had been built. The human prisoners were packed inside the fence, many watching the lightening horizon with what I could only guess was apprehension.

"Stay hidden up here, Tal," I said. "If I have to make a run for it, cover fire from your crossbow will help a lot."

Tal hunkered down on the roof and said, "You got it." As I turned away, he added, "Whack that trog upside the head once for me."

I moved along the rooftop, getting far away from Tal while keeping an eye on the camp. I came to an empty alley and jumped down into it. I slipped to the mouth of the alley and waited for the challenge. It wasn't long in coming.

"Humans!" a man's voice called. "Once again, the Great One will allow one of you to issue challenge to him. Who will face him in single combat? Who will represent humanity against the greatest warrior who has ever lived?"

Stepping out from the alley, I called out loudly, "I, Scout First Class David Rice, will challenge the Great One."

NO WEAPONS

There were four trogs loafing near the alley. They all jumped as if stung when my challenge rang out. Silence fell across the camp and all heads turned my way as I strode toward the man who spoke for the trog leader. I had expected a young man, maybe someone captured as a boy and raised among the trogs. This man was on the high end of middle-age, with thinning, gray hair, a full, white beard, and muscular build. It appeared he had done well for himself serving this Great One.

The penned humans stared at me in disbelief as I strode past. I gave them my brightest smile.

"Don't worry," I said, injecting as much confidence into my voice as possible, "Once I win this challenge, I'll have you out of there as quickly as possible."

The people in the pen began talking at once. Some of comments filtered out of the crowd. I heard "brave" several times and "foolhardy" even more often. I couldn't blame them. I'd probably have thought the same thing in their place.

Beyond the old man who spoke for the Great One stood a trog who must *be* the Great One. He was exceptionally tall for a trog—close to my own height—and looked like he was solid muscle. His body bore the scars of many battles. It was what I'd expected to see but would have been happy to have been proven wrong.

"You're the first man to come out of the city to issue challenge," said the man. "The Great One respects your courage and grants you the choice of weapons."

"Before I make that choice, could I ask some questions first?" I said.

"You may," he intoned.

"Do we fight to first blood, until one of the warriors concedes, or to the death?"

"The victor may show mercy if his opponent concedes. Do not count on receiving it," he responded.

"What happens if I win?" I asked.

The man laughed, "That will not happen."

"Humor me," I said.

"Should the impossible happen and you somehow defeat the Great One, you will be the new Great One, leader of all the trogs," he said.

"Prepare for new management, then," I said, loudly enough to be heard within the pen. "And what weapons do the trogs use in challenges among themselves?"

"They use only the weapons the gods granted them when they enter the world," he replied.

I unbuckled my sword belt and laid it on the ground.

I said, "Then I will fight the Great One as the trogs fight—hand-to-hand. No weapons."

WHO ARE YOU?

"**W**hy fight no weapons?"

It was the first thing the trog leader had said since I had arrived, but I recognized his voice. I'd first heard that voice when we were trapped in the cellar of the trading post. It was deep, rasping, and inhuman—a perfect match for the hulking trog standing before me.

"I must win as you won or your people might not obey me." I said.

The Great One chuffed once—a short laugh, I guessed—then seemed to lose interest in further talk. His human translator, on the other hand, gave me a hard stare.

"Who *are* you?" he asked.

"Is there any more to issuing challenge than what I've already done?" I asked, ignoring the translator's question. "Do I have to beat my breast, brag about all of the men I have slain and the women I have wooed, stuff like that?"

"No, there is no breast-beating or bragging required," the man said. "The only thing left for you to do is fight and die."

The man leaned close to me, speaking quietly and with an authority absent from his public proclamations, "If you could, please die quickly. I have quite a lot to do today and this spectacle has already taken up far too much of my time."

Now my curiosity was piqued. There was a lot more going on between the translator and the trog leader than met the eye. Who was the translator and how had he ended up with the trogs? I no longer thought he was a trog captive who had been kept alive to serve the Great One. There was no subservience in the man's voice or manner. Was the Great One just a necessary figurehead for the translator? What complications would I face if I defeated the Great One?

Was every conspiracy on this planet Gordian in complexity?

"A challenge has been issued!" called the man, once again using the more subservient tone. "Is the challenge accepted?"

"Yes," said the Great One.

I wrenched my attention back to the challenge. I had enough problems without adding the puzzle of the translator to the mix.

The translator backed away from me and called, "Fight!"

The Great One hunched down, spread his arms wide and charged.

HOW TROGS FIGHT

I got the idea the big trog expected me to run from him. Instead, I went for the unexpected and charged at the Great One. I couldn't play it safe and hope to win. The trog slowed for just a second, letting me know I'd made the right choice.

Just outside of the reach of the charging trog, I dove head first. I spun in the air and landed on my back. The dew-soaked grass was slick and I slid fast. The Great One had been ready to grapple with me and couldn't adjust to my surprise move. I slid under his grasping hands and between his legs. Pulling my knees up to my chest, I threw my arms back against the trog's shins. His balance thrown off, the Great One toppled forward. As he fell over me, I kicked up with both legs. My feet caught him in the stomach and launched him into a flip.

With a grunt of pain, the trog landed hard on his back. I rolled to my feet. The Great One rolled over onto his hands and knees, struggling to regain his feet. While he was defenseless, I darted in and kicked him in the face. His head snapped back and a howl of pain burst from his lips. I skipped away as the Great One rose to a crouch. Blood dripped from his nose and anger burned in his eyes.

Again, the Great One opened his arms wide and advanced, but he was much more cautious this time. It looked like trogs fought up close, grappling with each other. I guessed that was his plan for me. I was sure he could crush me with those long, powerful arms. I had to wear him down with hit and fade attacks. That would take time and, as a bonus, interfere with the translator's busy schedule.

I charged right at the now-cautious trog, dodged right just before he could grab me, and landed a blow to his ear. Again, I was dancing away before the big trog could react.

I landed two more quick hits before the Great One lost his patience and came at me in a full out charge. Again, I dodged before landing a punch where a man's left kidney would be. The Great One roared in pain. He may not have a kidney where I'd hit, but whatever was there was vital.

I was feeling good. The Great One not only hadn't hit me, he was flailing about with clumsy sweeps of his arms. He had no idea how to react to my style of fighting. As long as I kept moving and avoided his sweeping arms, I was sure I could wear the trog down.

I feinted and skipped away, frustrating the Great One even more. His lips were pulled back in a snarl of rage. I was preparing for another furious charge from the big trog when I sensed someone behind me.

"You asked how trogs fight," the translator said quietly. "It's time to find out."

He shoved me toward the angry trog. With a roar of triumph, the Great One wrapped his arms around me and squeezed.

FOUL BLOW

All I could see was blue skin as the Great One crushed me against his chest and pinned my arms against my side. Hot, fetid breath assaulted my nose as the trog roared. I breathed in short gasps, the best I could manage while in the Great One's deadly embrace. My feet still touched the ground but I had no leverage. Without it, I couldn't lift the trog off his feet or force him to fall backward.

I pounded my forehead into the trog's face, breaking his nose and blackening his eyes. He roared in pain but his relentless grip never broke. I tried stomping his feet but, after my first attempt, he lifted me off the ground. Then I tried kicking his shins, but he held fast and even tightened his grip.

Spots swam before my eyes as I struggled to remember my academy training in xenozoology, but nothing useful came to mind. I was sure I must have learned *something* at the academy that would help me survive this fight. And then I recalled something the academy martial arts instructor had taught us.

"Nature works pretty much the same throughout the galaxy," he'd said. "All twelve of the sentient, bipedal races are vulnerable in nearly identical ways. There just aren't many protected places in a bipedal body in which to put vital organs. Just remember, any place your body is vulnerable, chances are an alien biped is vulnerable there, too."

Remembering my punch to the kidney, I rammed my knee between the trog's legs.

The Great One's eyes rolled back and a strangled moan escaped. His grip eased and I took my first good breath in what seemed like years. My arms were still pinned, so I rammed my knee into the trog's groin a second time.

The trog's grip relaxed further and I was able to wriggle free of it. Now that I was free from the Great One's crushing grip, I put everything I had into a last kick between the trog's legs. With a howl, he reeled away from me and dropped to his knees, hands protecting his groin. I drew several great breaths and considered how to finish the fight.

"Foul blow," cried the man who had shoved me. "This human has broken the rules of engagement!"

Rules of engagement? What was such a formal military term doing in the vocabulary of a desert madman? I put the thought aside for examination later—after I finished the challenge.

The man screeched something in the trog tongue before turning back to me. He said, "Your actions condemn you. The challenge is forfeited."

The trogs closest to me raised their spears and advanced.

WHAT ARE YOU?

Sometimes events reduce your choices so severely that there is only one thing to do. I did it.

Boost!

I was becoming quite used to the feeling of invulnerability as adrenaline flooded my system and time seemed to slow. The trog translator was bending to grab my sword. I flashed across the two meters separating us and drew the sword even as his hand wrapped around the scabbard. I slashed his chest in passing as I rushed the closest trogs.

I was among the trogs before they could react, a deadly blur who was too close for spear attacks. I broke a trog's knee with a kick, slashed the shoulder of a trog to my right, then punched another in front of me. Spinning, I hacked off the arm of one who had been behind me. Never stopping, I fell backward into a roll, came up in front of a fifth trog, and drove my sword into his gut. Yanking the blade free, I whirled to face the attack that I knew must be coming from the rest of the trogs.

There was no attack. All around me, the trogs backed away, pointing and muttering.

The translator, blood flowing down his chest, stared at me, agape.

"Y-you're the one from the alley yesterday," he said.

Dropping Boost before it dropped me, I nodded.

"And it had to be you in the bar last night," he continued.

"You're leaving out the trap door in the desert trading post and your scouting party the day before that," I said.

"I shouldn't have asked *who* you are earlier," the translator said. "I should have asked *what* you are."

"I'm just a man," I said.

"How many have you killed?" he asked.

"Just trogs, or should I count the men who got in my way, too?" I asked. "And, if you don't want that number going up by one, you'll keep your mouth shut unless I give you permission to speak."

The translator's eyes widened.

"As the new leader of this trog army-" I began.

"No!" rasped the Great One, staggering to his feet. "Have not yielded."

Didn't this Great One know when to give up? Anger washed over me, building with each step as I stalked toward the swaying trog leader. Dropping my sword so there could be no question that I had fought hand-to-hand, I slugged the Great One with an uppercut to the chin. His eyes rolled back and he fell backward, landing with a thud.

I glared at the trogs surrounding me and yelled, "*Now* he yields."

FIFTEEN YEARS

My proclamation was echoing from the buildings surrounding the park when the penned prisoners began cheering. That was a pleasant change from the translator's I-hope-you-die-screaming-in-agony glower. The trogs were silent, milling about, unsure how to respond to my unexpected victory.

Retrieving my sword, I walked over to the translator. I smiled broadly into his glower.

"Do you have any idea," he said, "how long it took me to insinuate myself into trog society? To learn their vile language? To manipulate them into this campaign?"

"Why, no, I don't know," I said. "You know what else? I don't care."

"Fifteen years, that's how long! Fifteen years feigning subservience to these brutes. Fifteen years of humiliation at their hands. All for *this* invasion of Mordan," he cried. "And you ruined all of my work in fifteen minutes."

"You're giving me too much credit," I said. "Our airship crashed in the city yesterday afternoon. So, really, it's more like fifteen hours."

The translator's face went purple with rage. With a bellow, he took a swing at my jaw. I stepped aside, grabbed his wrist, and flipped him onto his back.

Standing over the translator, I said, "As the new leader of this army of trogs, I order them to go home and disperse."

I waved toward the trogs, "Translate that order for them."

The translator stood and shouted something in the trog language. The trogs hefted their spears and turned toward the human prisoners. The cheering within the pen died as the trogs closed in.

I smashed the translator's head with the pommel of my sword. He fell in a heap as I ran toward the prisoners. I dodged through the trogs, ready to Boost if any of them attacked me or tried to block my path. None did. Maybe they thought I was leading the attack. Maybe they were too afraid of me to lift a spear against me.

Breaking through the ranks of advancing trogs, I held my hands up and willed the trogs to stop.

"No," I shouted, waving my arms. "I didn't order this. Go back!"

The only trog who understood human speech lay unconscious twenty meters away. The only human who spoke trog couldn't be trusted to speak to the trogs, even if he had been conscious. And the approaching trogs didn't understand a word I said. For all I know, they thought I was urging them on. Or maybe they thought I was crazy. But hundreds of trogs bore down on the captive citizens of Faroon.

AN UNEXPECTED ARRIVAL

The screams of terrified people filled my ears. The advancing trogs, spears lowered, filled my vision. The threat of Boost Burnout filled my mind. The sorrow that I would never see Callan again filled my heart.

Above the screams, I could hear the roaring of my blood, ready for one last Boost.

A few meters to my left, a trog stumbled and pitched forward. One in front of me dropped his spear and clutched his arm. A third toppled backward.

All along the advancing line, trogs screamed and fell as crossbow bolts rained out of the brightening morning sky. The roaring I'd heard over the screams hadn't been my blood, after all. Vibrations shook my insides as I looked up.

A shadow fell across me as Martin Bane's airship rumbled overhead,. Martin leaned against the rail, directing the firing of at least two dozen of his crew. They fired crossbows in rotating volleys, keeping a steady stream of quarrels raining down on the trogs. His airship was so low I could count the rings on Martin's fingers. His fleet flew in formation to either side of his ship. Each of the other airships also had rows of airmen firing crossbows.

Bane spotted me and sketched a salute, all the while keeping his attention on the firing line.

"Drive 'em back, lads!" he called. "And watch out for that young man waving the sword about like a fool. Her Highness will be quite put out if we damage him."

Confused, frightened, many of them wounded, the trogs were driven back by the aerial onslaught. The two outer flanks of airships pulled ahead of the others, encircling the trogs and driving them into a packed mass at the center of the park. One trog finally made a big show of throwing down his spear and dropped to his knees. Those around him followed his lead and it spread until all of the trogs knelt, unarmed, inside the circle of airships.

"Cease fire!" Bane bellowed.

The airmen stopped shooting but they all kept their crossbows cocked and trained on the trogs.

I ran over to the Great One. He was groaning but was still laying where I'd left him just a few minutes before.

"Get up," I said, grabbing his arm and pulling. "Now, tell your army to put their hands on their heads and wait for further orders."

The big trog spoke and the trogs did as I'd instructed.

I looked around, trying to spot the translator. I didn't see him anywhere. In all the confusion, the translator had escaped.

PUDDLE OF BLOOD

"You look like you've lost something, Rice," Bane called from above.

"Not some*thing*, some*one*. A man who was working with the trogs and speaks their language," I said. "He's got steel gray hair, a white beard, and was bare-chested. Can you see anyone like that from up there?"

Bane and some of his crewmen looked, but it was a futile hope. The park and town square were filled with people looking for loved ones, shouting thanks to the airship crews, jeering at the trogs, and crying for lost loved ones. Besides, it was probable the translator had run into the city. He could be hiding anywhere by now. I had no illusions that Bane would find him.

"No sign of anyone matching your description," Bane said, after a few minutes, "but I'll have my crew keep watch."

I had a feeling allowing the translator to get away would come back to haunt me, but I'd deal with him if he ever turned up again. I had far more things to worry about right now.

"Drop a line and come on down," I told Bane. "We've got some planning to do."

After Bane and some of his men were down, I said, "You cut it a little close there at the end. Did it really take you that long to defeat the trog airships?"

"It wasn't an easy job, Rice. We had to find ways to beat the trogs without harming the human crews on the airships," Bane said. "It took a while, but I thought it was what Her Highness would want."

"I can safely say Callan will be pleased with your actions, both against the airships and against the trogs," I said. "Mentioning Callan, I need to let her know everything worked out. I've got a crossbowman on a nearby rooftop who can take word to her. His name is Tal. Can you send someone to get him?"

Bane picked a crewman and I told him where to find Tal.

As the crewman ran off, Bane asked, "Have you got any idea what you're going to do with all those trogs?"

"Yes, tell now," said the Great One.

"I'm going to send them home and have them return to their tribes," I said. "They'll be unarmed and escorted by some of our airships."

"As long as the escorts will continue to receive the same pay rate, there won't be any problems," Bane said.

I turned to the Great One, "As for you, if you ever lead an army against humans again, I will personally kill you and have any who follow you hunted down like animals."

"Warrior's threat. You make good Great One," the trog said. He started walking toward the sitting trogs, "I tell them."

We were turning back to our planning when we spotted Bane's crewman returning at a run.

"I checked the roof," he said, gasping. "All I found was a puddle of blood."

THE RETURN OF GORT

Bane and some of his men came with me to check out the scene on the rooftop. The puddle of blood lay right where Tal had been kneeling when last I saw him. The blood had to be Tal's, but who had attacked him and why had they taken Tal with them?

"Everyone spread out and look for a club or something similar. It will have blood stains on it," I said.

"Wouldn't the attacker have kept his weapon?" Bane asked.

"Not if all he had was a club," I said. "Tal had a sword and crossbow, nice upgrades over a big stick."

One of Bane's crew found the blood-stained club on the ground below the roof and it told the whole story. It was one of the table legs Sarn had used to fight the trogs last night. Only one person had been in the bar when we'd left.

Gort.

"I know who attacked Tal," I said. "I'm sure the guy enjoyed clubbing Tal, but I'm his real target."

"You seem to make enemies everywhere you go, Rice. Maybe you should work on your people skills," Bane said. "What did you do to irritate this guy?"

"I ruined his little gang, which included Tal at the time. Then

Tal whacked him with a chair and came over to my side," I said. "Tal knows where we've been hiding and Gort strikes me as the viciously persuasive type of thug. I've got to make sure Callan is safe. We can search for Tal after that."

"Want me to come with you?" Bane asked. "Or some of my men?"

"No," I sighed. "The situation between the trogs and humans isn't stable. All it takes is one person deciding to get a little revenge and we'd have a massacre on our hands. I need you to keep it under control."

Bane nodded, then surprised me by pulling my Onesie out of his pocket.

"If you're going to go alone, you'd better take this," he said. At my incredulous look, he grinned, "It wasn't ruined, just depleted. And in pieces. Yes, I lied. Raider, remember?"

Pocketing the gun, I ran off. As I got closer to the hiding place, I scanned for blood or signs of a struggle. I didn't see anything, but that didn't mean anything. I had to assume Gort had gotten here ahead of me.

At the door, I tapped out the signal we'd agreed on and then pushed the door open.

Gort sat against the far wall, Tal's crossbow aimed at me. Raoul was nowhere to be seen.

"It's him," Gort said.

Raoul's voice came from my left, probably from the corner nearest the door, "Shoot him!"

GOT HIM

The scene inside the hiding place seared into my brain. Tristan, Nist, Milo, Sarn, and Tal sat huddled against the far wall, hands bound behind their backs and eyes wide. Milo's sister Kim lay in the small bed beside them, her hands tied to the bed. She watched it all through heavy-lidded eyes. Gort crouched in the left corner, a feral grin splitting his face as the crossbow tracked toward me. Raoul was somewhere to the left of the doorway. I didn't see Callan at all. Raoul was probably holding a knife at her throat.

My sole advantage was that neither Raoul nor Gort had seen me Boost. Raoul had heard about it, but he'd run away before I Boosted in the alley.

Boost!

The *twang* of the crossbow stretched as time slowed. I fell backward, raising my hands as if to ward off the bolt. I caught the bolt just before it struck my head. I cried out as if I'd been hit, masking the sound as I snapped the bolt in two.

Dropping Boost, I lay on the ground, twitching and thrashing as if suffering the throes of death. The movement distracted Gort as I scraped the bolt tip across my forehead, just above my right eye. Blood welled and ran profusely, as head cuts always do, and I held the back end of the bolt over my right eye. I hid the bolt tip against my left forearm then let that arm flop to the ground. I kept my left eye open and stared at a spot on the ceiling.

"Well, what happened?" asked Raoul.

"Got him through the eye," Gort crowed, hopping up and capering about.

From the left, I heard Callan moan as Raoul said, "Stop celebrating and make sure he's dead."

Gort approached cautiously and saw just what he expected to see. He grabbed my foot and dragged me into the room. I kept my stare unfocused.

"*David!*" Callan shrieked.

Raoul had been holding a knife to her throat but he let it drop when he saw me. Callan broke free from his grip and dropped to my side. Perfect. She was blocking the view of both the prince and the thug.

I thrust the bolt tip into her hand and whispered, "Stab Raoul or Gort. I'll take it from there."

HE MEANS SOMETHING ELSE

Raoul grabbed Callan's arm and pulled her back against the wall. Right next to him.

"That is enough, Callan," he said. "These histrionics over the death of a mere guard are beneath you. A woman of your station must stand aloof from the petty concerns of your subjects."

"You are an insufferable prig, Raoul. I will make you pay for all that you have done to me and mine," Callan said. "In pain and blood, I will make you pay."

Callan stabbed the crossbow tip into Raoul's thigh and then twisted the shaft after it had sliced through muscle. Raoul screamed as blood soaked his pants leg. Callan spun away from him and he fell to the floor.

Gort, who had cocked and reloaded the crossbow, raised it to take a shot. The whine of the Onesie echoed in the small room as I fired from the hip. My hasty shot hit Gort's crossbow and it exploded into a thousand pieces. Splinters ripped into Gort's face and neck. Gort opened his mouth to scream and blood gushed from it. He fell back into the corner, his body quivering as his life drained onto the floor.

Raoul was rolling back and forth holding his wounded leg, his face white with pain, when I pressed my sword to his throat.

A line of blood welled under my blade as I said, "Please, Raoul, give me an excuse to end this. Any excuse at all."

Raoul's knife clattered on the floor and I swept it away with my foot, sighing, "I guess you're not as stupid as I thought, Raoul. What a pity."

Callan picked up Raoul's knife and set to cutting the bonds holding our friends.

Tristan came straight over to tend to Raoul's leg. He was rubbing his wrists and shaking his hands, trying to get feeling back in them.

"Bring my bag, Nist. I'll remove the shaft once my hands stop tingling." Gesturing toward Gort's still-jerking body, he added, "Milo, cover the body with a spare blanket."

Once all the bonds had been cut, Callan ran to me and wrapped her arms around me. She pulled me close and kissed me hard.

"Don't you ever scare me like that again," she said, tears streaming down her cheeks and soaking into my shirt.

I held her tightly and said, "As you wish."

In a stage whisper, Milo said, "Kim, he keeps saying that to her but I think he means something else. Am I right?"

"Oh yeah, Milo, you're right," Kim replied in another stage whisper.

"Then why doesn't he just say what he means?" Milo asked.

Why indeed?

I looked into Callan's eyes, still shining with tears, and said, "I know very little about your country, Callan, but Mordan claims my heart because it claims your heart. Mordan holds my oath because you hold my oath. Mordan is my country because it is your country.

"Callan Debah Lois Antrulta Ziliah Villas, my life has no meaning without you. My heart has no purpose without you. I love you," I said. "Will you marry me?"

WISER ADVICE

Leave it to Raoul to spoil the proposal I'd been rehearsing for the last two days.

"Idiot!" said Raoul through clenched teeth. "Callan is betrothed to a Tartegian prince. She would never give that up for the likes of *yargh!*"

"Oh, I am sorry, Prince Raoul," Tristan spoke in a monotone. "My hand slipped. It's probably because the ropes you used to tie us up cut off the blood flow to my hands. I do hope that didn't hurt."

"Raoul, your counsel is neither sought nor desired," Callan said. "I have already received far wiser advice on this matter than you could ever give."

"When could you have receive that?" I asked. "I *just* popped the question."

"Days ago, under the city of Beloren," Callan said.

I remembered Rob pulling Callan close and speaking softly to her just before he gave me his sword. "Do you mean Rob's last words to you?"

Callan nodded, "Yes, that's when he gave me his advice."

I said, "But he had already made his opinion *extremely* clear when we kissed on the airship, back before the sandstorm hit."

"He hadn't known you very long then," Callan said. "You'd been with us less than a day and had spent a lot of that time sleeping."

"That's true, but he hadn't known me very much longer when he died," I said.

"Rob always was a shrewd judge of character, David. You impressed him, and Rob wasn't a man who was easily impressed." Callan looked into my eyes. "What he told me was 'Marry Rupor if you must. Marry David if you can.'"

Out of the corner of my eye, I saw Raoul open his mouth. Tristan shoved a liquor bottle into Raoul's mouth and turned the bottle up.

"So, which is it? 'Must' or 'can'?" I asked.

Callan's lips spread into a smile and she said, "Can."

Our friends cheered so loudly we couldn't even hear Raoul's outraged sputtering. Not that I was trying to hear him. I was too busy kissing my future wife.

"David Rice?" a voice rose over the cheering.

One of Bane's men stood in the doorway.

"How did you find us?" I asked.

"I ain't deaf, son," he said, motioning at our cheering friends. "Cap'n sends his compliments and requests you join him at the town square."

"What's happening?" I asked, fearing riots or worse.

"Cap'n put ships out on scout duty after we won the air battle," the man said. "One of the scouts is steaming back to the city with a Tartegian warship on its tail."

TARTEGIANS

Damn the Tartegians. I didn't even get to finish kissing Callan.

"Tal, how are you feeling?" I asked, still holding my bride-to-be close.

"I'm okay," he said. "Gort didn't hit anything important—just my head."

"Then you're in charge of Raoul. You won't need brains for that; just keep him quiet and out of sight," I said. "I don't care how you do it, just don't do any permanent damage to him."

Tal grinned and gave a mock salute. Raoul sputtered with more outrage, which made me smile.

To Bane's crewman, I said, "Please get some more men and get rid of that body."

The crewman gave a much better salute than Tal and left.

"Tristan, do you need anything?" I asked.

"I'm fine, lad," he said, "though Nist could use some help mending my airship. We'll want the *Pauline* air-worthy so we can take Her Highness on the last leg of her journey home."

"I'll see how many men Bane can spare," I said. "Milo, come with us in case we need to send a message back here."

Milo grinned, falling in behind us as I took Callan's hand.

The park was bustling when we arrived. Bane had men guarding the trogs, men tending the sick and wounded citizens, and men patrolling the streets of the city.

"What news have you got for us?" I called.

Bane turned, his eyes immediately tracking to our clasped hands.

Arching an eyebrow, he said, "I suspect you're the one with the news. Am I correct in assuming congratulations are in order? Do you think her father will approve? And, of the utmost importance, do I get to kiss the bride-to-be?"

"When my father hears what David has done *for* me," Callan smiled, tilting her cheek so Bane could plant a kiss, "and what Raoul and his mother have done *to* me, I think he'll come around."

A shadow passed over us as the scout ship drifted up. It dropped lines to crewmen on the ground but the crew stayed at their stations, all eyes on the pursuing airship. The Tartegian warship came up close behind the scout ship, armed men crowding its rails.

An officer stood in the bow and, his voice booming, called, "We seek the man called Martin Bane. I hold a royal order for his arrest."

SHOOT HIM NOW!

"Captain," Callan called, "why is a Tartegian warship attempting to enforce a Mordanian royal order? For that matter, why is a Tartegian warship in Mordanian skies at all? You are allowed in our skies to escort royalty, nothing more."

Murmurs of assent rose from the people in the park, all of whom had stopped to watch this drama play out.

"I am not in the habit of explaining my actions or my orders to random young women," the officer said, contempt in his voice. "Now, if you please, direct me to the *man* in charge, young woman."

Conversation in the park died away at this response. That meant my next words were heard by all.

"The proper form of address to this young lady is 'Your Highness.' Further, I will hear a proper tone of respect in your voice when next you speak or you will answer to my blade!"

Callan crossed her arms and did something I would have sworn was impossible if I hadn't seen it for myself. She looked *down* on a man floating twenty-five meters above her.

"That was a nice touch, David," she said quietly. "It's going to be fun having you around."

"Princess Callan?" the officer exclaimed. "Can it truly be you?

You've been missing so long that some in the palace have begun to fear the worst. Prince Rupor, of course, is not among those."

Around us, voices rose again, this time in excited speculation and amazement. The kidnapped princess had turned up in their city and appeared to have had a hand in defeating the trogs. Listening to snippets of conversation, I could tell a legend had just been born. How long would it be before the story had Callan, sword waving above her head, leading the final charge against the trogs?

"You have not answered my question, Captain," Callan said.

"Of course, Your Highness," the captain said. I'll give him this, he got the tone right this time. "I'll be right down."

As the crew scrambled to lower their captain, Bane said, "What is your intention, Highness?"

"Have no fear, Martin," Callan said, "I will honor our agreement. You will not be turned over to this Tartegian."

"I had no doubts on that score, Highness," Bane said, "but if you expect a fight I must signal for my men to get into position."

"Forgive me for misinterpreting your concern, Martin. I do not expect a fight," Callan said.

The captain marched up to Callan and bowed. "Captain Hanral at your service, Your Highness. I am pleased to find you safe and well. To answer your question, we enforce the standing order of arrest issued by your father."

"And how long has that order been standing, Captain?" Callan asked.

"I am sorry, Your Highness," Hanral said, "I don't know exactly. I believe the order was issued the day after your abduction."

"Thank you, Captain Hanral. You may disregard that order," Callan said.

"I don't understand," Hanral said. "Don't you want those responsible for your kidnapping brought to justice?"

"More than you can possibly imagine, Captain," Callan said. Motioning to Bane, she added, "But Martin Bane has rendered invaluable service to Mordan and is no longer subject to arrest."

"This man is Martin Bane?" Hanral's eyes went wide.

Martin sketched a salute, "I'm so very pleased to meet you, Captain Hanral."

The captain jumped back from Bane and shouted to his crew, "Shoot this man. Shoot him now!"

SEEKING PRINCE RAOUL

My heart stopped as Callan jumped in front of Bane and shouted to the Tartegian crewmen, "You will do no such thing."

Then I jumped in front of Callan. To my immense relief, the Tartegian crewmen were already lowering their crossbows. Spinning to face Callan, I said, "Don't *do* that!"

Hanral, his face pale, added, "I must concur with your bodyguard, Your Highness."

"Well, *I* appreciate the gesture, Your Highness," Martin said. I glared at him over Callan's head and he added, "But it was rather ill conceived."

Callan, unflustered by all the commotion, turned her gaze back to Hanral. "Listen to me very carefully, Captain. I am countermanding the standing order for Martin's arrest. As of this moment it is null and void. Is that clear?"

"But Your Highness," Hanral said, "this order comes from your king. A princess cannot countermand her king."

"You *dare* to argue Mordanian law with *me*?" Callan's eyes blazed. Once again, she managed to look down upon a man who stood a full head taller than she. "You are in command of a foreign warship in Mordanian skies. Wars have begun over less. If you want to argue legalities, Captain, let's start with an explanation for that."

All thoughts of arresting Martin Bane appeared to flee from the captain's mind. Callan had neatly taken Hanral off the offensive and put him on defense.

"W-w-why I carry royal permits to sail Mordan's skies," Hanral stammered. "The permits, like the arrest order, are signed by your father. Our squadron escorted Prince Rupor to Morda and His Highness offered us to aid in the search for you, Your Highness. That is why we sail Mordan's skies."

"I see," Callan appeared to mull over the captain's answer. "You will fetch those permits when this conversation is over."

"Of course, Your Highness," Hanral replied.

"But that doesn't explain what you're doing here in Faroon," she added.

"Ah, that is easily explained, Your Highness," the captain beamed, apparently happy to have a ready answer. "We had returned to Morda to deliver a message to Prince Rupor and your father. While we were there, word came that Faroon may have been attacked. As the city was along the route back to the squadron, Prince Rupor suggested that we investigate the situation. Your father accepted his offer."

"Very well, Captain," Callan relented, "your explanation is reasonable. Have those permits brought to me and then you can be on your way to rejoin your squadron."

"Thank you, Your Highness," the captain said. "I do have one question for you, if I may?"

"Of course," Callan said.

"You are not the only person we seek," Hanral said. "We also seek Prince Raoul. Do you know where he could be found?"

A LOSS FOR WORDS

"Prince Raoul was with us when our airship crashed in Faroon," Callan said. "I'm afraid we were separated shortly after that. Now that the city is once again under human control, the prince is our top priority."

Hanral's face fell, though he rallied to say, "I'm certain you will do your best, Your Highness."

"You have my word, Captain Hanral. We will not leave Faroon without Prince Raoul," Callan said. "Now, please do not let me stop you from rejoining your squadron."

"Thank you, Your Highness," the captain said. "but that won't be necessary. All ships in my squadron have a standing order from Prince Rupor that overrides all others. Should any Tartegian ship find you or His Highness, we are to render assistance and provide escort to Morda."

I was cursing silently but Callan gave the captain a dazzling smile. "That's very kind of you and Prince Rupor. Now, could you fetch those permits your mentioned? It's important that my subjects see me verify their authenticity."

"At once, Your Highness," Hanral said.

After the captain was hoisted back to his airship, Bane asked, "What really happened with the Spare Prince?"

"He ran away the first chance he got," I said.

"And are you really going to take the time to search for him?" Bane said.

"Don't have to," I said. "We've got him tied up in a hideout not far from here. Tristan is looking after him."

"Isn't he a little old to be watching someone like Raoul?" Bane asked.

"Sorry, I wasn't clear," I said. "It turns out Tristan is a doctor. He's tending to Raoul's wounded leg."

"The trogs got him after he ran?" Bane said. "Good for them."

"No," Callan said. "I stabbed him."

Bane's mouth opened and closed twice but no words came out. It was the first time I'd seen Bane at a loss for words. Taking advantage of his silence, I told him the highlights of our time in Faroon.

"I've got no idea how we're going to keep the Tartegians from taking Raoul on their warship," I said, "but we most definitely do not want Raoul talking to any Tartegians before we get Callan home."

"Don't worry, darling," Callan said, "I've already figured that out. Milo? I want you to deliver a message to Tristan."

As Callan gave her message to Milo, I decided to have one last talk with the Great One. I wanted to ask him about the translator. By the time I returned, Milo had delivered the message and was back, also.

"Remember the human translator for the trogs?" I said. "The Great One says the plan to form an army and invade Mordan was concocted by the translator."

"Does this translator have a name?" Bane asked.

"I only know what the trogs called him," I replied. "I had a hard time understanding what the Great One said, but it was something like Hard Hand Wind Low."

Callan cried, "Ardan Windslow?"

Bane exclaimed, "It can't be. He's dead!"

WINDSLOW

"You both knew this man?" I asked. "Who is he?"

Bane bowed to Callan, gesturing for her to speak first.

"You remember the kidnapping attempt I told you about?" she asked. "When I was four and Rob earned the sword he gave to you?"

"Of course," I said. "Was Windslow one of the nobles behind the plot?"

"No, it's worse than that. Windslow was captain of the palace guard. At one time, he'd even been my uncle's personal bodyguard. My father trusted Windslow absolutely," Callan said. "The lords behind the plot bribed him to clear the path for the kidnappers. He changed guard schedules, moved guards to other positions, and bribed or threatened other guards.

"After the conspirators were discovered, those lords tried to lay most of the blame on Windslow. It didn't work and every one of them was executed, with the exception of Windslow. Somehow, he managed to escape the dungeon with the help of some petty criminal."

Comprehension dawned as another tale came to mind.

"Martin, are you the 'petty criminal' in Callan's tale?" I asked.

Callan whipped around in surprise, catching Bane's slow nod.

"We were kept in the same cell," he said. "Windslow had an escape plan, but it took two men. I was awaiting execution so of course I agreed to help. Once we were free, Windslow went to a bar in one of the poorest areas in the city. He told me he needed to arrange passage out of the country for the two of us. Windslow had me keep watch from an alley. After an hour of waiting, I went looking for him. I found his headless body in a back room."

"Are you sure it was him?" I asked.

"I didn't take time to investigate," Bane said. "The corpse had the right clothes and the right build. The head was missing, but I assumed it was Windslow and that he'd given himself away. It looks like I was fooled."

Callan said, "The lords always claimed Windslow recruited *them*, though no one believed it. I guess Martin wasn't the only one fooled by Windslow."

"Is it possible Windslow was working with Tarteg at the time?" I asked.

"There were rumors... Tarteg and Mordan have a long history of conflict," Callan said. "But I was too young to understand any of that. It was sixteen years ago, after all."

"Whatever drove Windslow to betray your family back then seems to still be driving him today," I said. "It can't be a coincidence that you were kidnapped just as Windslow decided to attack Mordan. But was Windslow working with Raoul's mother? Or does he just have a good spy network and decided to take advantage of the situation?"

Callan's face hardened, "Either way, all of this has only been possible because of my betrothal to Rupor."

MOSTLY UNHARMED

"Everyone told me Queen Beatrice—Raoul's mother—was the one who suggested joining the kingdoms through marriage. It seems she waited until she had everything in place for her plot before making that suggestion," Callan said. "I thought the marriage would mean an end to war between our countries. Instead, it's caused more death and destruction."

"But why would she want the trogs to attack?" I asked. "How would that help turn Raoul into a hero?"

"Maybe her goal was to lure Rupor into combat," Bane said. "If Rupor dies, Raoul goes from Spare Prince to Heir Prince in the blink of an eye. That's one heck of a display of motherly love, don't you think?"

"This is giving me a headache," I said. "I'm changing the subject for a while. Martin, can you send some men to repair Tristan's airship? Milo can lead them to the *Pauline*."

"Consider it done," Martin said. He turned and began rounding up a repair team.

Callan said. "Milo, we need you to lead a repair crew to our airship. Head back to Tristan after that. Please deliver another message to him."

Callan whispered in Milo's ear for a few seconds. Milo grinned, saluted, then headed off with the crew. The salute wasn't bad for a kid who'd never given one in his life.

"Now what?" I asked.

"Now we're going to make Captain Hanral the happiest man in the city," Callan said. Raising her voice, she called, "Please tell Captain Hanral I've just received word that Prince Raoul has been found."

That caused some activity on the Tartegian airship. Within seconds, Hanral was lowered to the ground. Despite the excitement, the captain was carrying several pieces of paper. They must be the permits Callan had asked to see.

"You have news of His Highness?" Hanral asked.

"Yes, Captain. Raoul is alive and mostly unharmed," Callan said. "He's with-"

"*Mostly* unharmed?" Hanral interrupted. "What does that mean?"

Callan folded her arms and glared at the captain. Hanral had no idea why Callan was displeased. I decided to take pity on the guy.

"Pardon the Captain's *interruption*, Your Highness," I said. "I'm sure his concern for Prince Raoul's health and welfare overrode proper etiquette."

"Y-yes, that is exactly it," the captain bowed. "I humbly beg your pardon, Your Highness."

"Your dedication to Prince Raoul is commendable, Captain," Callan relented. "You need not concern yourself. Raoul has a leg wound, painful but nothing to worry about. We travel with a physician who is attending to Raoul's wound now."

"Please forgive me, Your Highness," Hanral said, "but I must insist my ship's surgeon examine His Highness."

A FINE IDEA

"But of course, Captain. I'd expect nothing less from a dedicated officer such as yourself," Callan said, smiling. "I'm sure Dr. Agrilla will welcome a second opinion."

"Dr. Agrilla?" Hanral asked. "The man they call the Desert Doctor?"

"The very same," Callan said. "Is there a problem?"

"No. Not one bit," the captain said. "From all reports I've heard, Prince Raoul couldn't be in more capable hands."

"Splendid," Callan clapped her hands in delight. "Then you won't mind if Raoul stays on our ship, with his doctor?"

The captain was taken aback, "You won't be riding on my airship, Your Highness?"

"I began my return journey on Dr. Agrilla's airship," Callan said. "I'll finish it the same way."

Captain Hanral took a moment to think the situation through, balancing Tristan's reputation and a possible perceived insult to the woman he thought would be his future queen against the need to insure Raoul's survival.

"I'll defer to my surgeon. If he has no objections to His Highness riding with your doctor then I will allow it," Hanral said.

"That's a fine idea, Captain," Callan said. "Have your surgeon fetched and I'll take you to Raoul."

The captain turned to call instructions to his airship. I took a moment to pull Callan away from Hanral.

"Callan, we can't allow Raoul to talk to the surgeon or Captain Hanral," I whispered. "He'll tell them who stabbed him, for one thing, and-"

Callan placed a finger over my lips, "Raoul won't tell them anything. Milo is delivering instructions to Tristan to drug Raoul. He'll be incoherent at worst, unconscious at best."

"That's...brilliant. Our children are going to be smart *and* beautiful," I said. "But what are they going to get from me?"

"Courage, strength, conviction, quick wits, a level head in emergencies," Callan said. "I could go on, but the good Captain is looking our way."

We rejoined the captain and, soon, his surgeon joined us. Together, we set off for our hiding place. I only hoped Raoul was unconscious when we got there.

IN YOUR DEBT

Raoul's eyes were wide open when we reached the hiding place. When I walked in, his eyes swung toward me. Then they tracked past me to a spot on the wall. It looked as if Raoul was struggling to control his vision but not having much success. His eyes fluttered and then shut before Captain Hanral or the surgeon entered.

Tristan met the surgeon as he entered and the two quickly fell into a jargon-filled conversation. I got the gist of the conversation, if not the details.

"The surgeon seems impressed," I murmured to Callan. "It's good to know Tristan is as good as his reputation."

After exclaiming over the skill of Tristan's work, the surgeon asked, "Why is His Highness unconscious, Dr. Agrilla? I would have used a local anesthesia."

"As would I," Tristan said, "but Prince Raoul insisted I save that for the city's wounded. He put those people ahead of his own suffering. I gave His Highness a glass of liquor to help calm him. When he wasn't looking, I mixed a few choice drugs in with the whiskey. Knocked him right out."

"Very clever, Dr. Agrilla," the surgeon said. "Prince Raoul's bravery should be an inspiration to us all."

"I think I'm going to hurl," I whispered to Callan.

"You are so angry you wish to throw something?" Callan whispered back.

"Uh, no. It's old Terran slang, something I learned from my grandfather," I whispered. "It means to throw up, as if something were making you sick to your stomach."

"Hurl," Callan tried the word on for size. "It is much shorter than 'hugging the chamber pot.' I like it."

The surgeon addressed Captain Hanral, "Prince Raoul is in excellent hands, Captain. I see no reason why he shouldn't ride with the good doctor."

"All of Tarteg is in your debt, Dr. Agrilla," Hanral said. "Please let us know if you are in need of any medical supplies for the trip to Morda."

Hanral turned to Callan, "With your permission, Your Highness, I'll return to my airship and prepare her for escort duty."

"Of course, Captain," Callan said. "We'll leave once the *Pauline* is repaired."

GOING HOME

Once the Tartegians were gone, Callan addressed everyone, "Are you all ready for a trip to the palace? My father will want to thank each of you personally."

Milo was the first to respond, "Are there girls my age in the palace?"

"There are quite a few young ladies at court," Callan smiled. "I'm sure they will find a veteran of the trog war quite fascinating."

Milo grinned, "I'm in."

"I believe you already planned for Nist and me to accompany you," Tristan said, "and I wouldn't miss this for the world. But I must insist we take Kim, as well. She's still under my care."

"Of course Kim is coming with us," Callan said. "Tal? Sarn?"

"Nah," Tal said. Sarn elbowed him. "I mean, no Your Highness. Now that the trogs are gone, Sarn and me got to help get the city going again. And we got to tell a bunch of people that Gort won't be a problem no more."

Callan kissed each one on the cheek. "Take care of yourselves."

"Tristan," I said, "we'll send some crewmen over to help move Kim and the Spare Prince. Milo, stay with your sister."

As Callan and I headed back to the park, I asked, "Have you figured out what to do with Martin?"

"He has to come with us," Callan said. "The rest of the airships might cut and run if it looked like we were leaving their commander behind. Besides, I don't want someone shooting him for the bounty my father is bound to have set for him."

"You don't think it might be a bit, I don't know, startling to everyone at the palace for Martin to be on deck with us?" I asked.

"It will, but I'll be there to keep everyone calm and to explain the situation," Callan said. "Have I ever told you that you worry too much?"

"That's my job—it says so right in the description," I said.

Callan linked arms with me, "Then far be it from me to ruin your fun. Worry to your heart's content, darling."

Martin and Callan finalized their plans for the trogs and the disposition of the mercenary fleet, then Martin issued the necessary orders. He put his first mate in command of his airship and we went to the *Pauline*. Repairs were completed moments later and we all boarded the little airship.

Nist took the controls and the *Pauline* rose into the sky above Faroon. The Tartegian warship swung in front of us and the two airships set course for Morda.

The princess was finally going home.

APPROACHING THE PALACE

It was a lovely day for a flight, even if Raoul did wake up a few hours into the voyage. Callan and I stayed on deck, as far from Raoul as possible. More bothersome, with a Tartegian warship nearby, our behavior had to be circumspect. We could talk about anything we wanted, but we couldn't even risk holding hands. The last thing we needed was a Tartegian airman spotting us behaving in a romantic manner toward each other.

The sun lay close to the horizon when Morda came into view. The city sprawled across the horizon, far larger than any city I'd seen since my crash landing. Martin opened a small chest he'd left on deck and withdrew a flag.

Callan clapped her hands and said, "Wherever did you get that, Martin?"

Hoisting the flag, Martin said, "I spoke with the Lord of Faroon—decent chap, by the way—and he was happy to let me borrow one of the flags the city's naval squadron keeps on hand."

The flag showed Callan's family crest—a golden falcon preying on a green field—with a gold tiara above the hawk.

"I'm guessing that flag tells the world you're aboard this ship?" I said.

Callan nodded, giving Martin a dazzling smile.

Callan pointed to a vast and magnificent palace atop a low hill, directing Nist to land there. "But can you make the approach at low altitude and down that wide boulevard? It was designed with low flying airships in mind. I want my people to see that I'm safe. Martin, go below and get Raoul ready to leave the ship. I want him walking, so get him a crutch if he needs it."

Nist brought the ship in low, no more than fifty feet above the ground. Based on the cheering as we approached the city, Callan's flag had been spotted and word had raced through the city ahead of us. Heads poked out of windows and people thronged the street below. Callan, now standing in the bow, was visible to all. She waved and laughed and cried as her people welcomed her home.

Cheering crowds followed the airship up the boulevard, chanting, singing, and calling out good wishes to Callan. If her people loved her this much, I couldn't wait to see her reception at the palace.

CAPTAIN HUNTER

At the palace docks, guards hurried to form ranks and palace functionaries ran about, preparing for the return of the princess. Our arrival was so unexpected, Nist docked the airship before the king and queen arrived on the scene.

A uniformed man bounded up the docking stairs, meeting Callan with a broad smile and a snappy salute. A dozen guards followed him.

"The whole country rejoices at your safe return, Your Highness!" he said.

"Thank you, Captain Hunter," Callan replied. "Are my parents on their way?"

"They should be here any second," Hunter said as gaze swept across those of us on deck. "Where is Captain Vonsteader?"

"Rob gave his life protecting me," Callan said. "This is David Rice, my new captain of the guard."

Hunter frowned, "I don't recall that name among your guardsmen, Your Highness."

"David was not a member of the guard. He saved Rob and me when trogs set upon us in the desert," Callan said.

Hunter's frown deepened.

"Rob personally took his oath," Callan said, "and David has saved my life half a dozen times since."

Hunter's frown did not change.

"And with his dying breath, Rob gave his sword to David," Callan continued.

The frown vanished and a hand shot out to grip mine, "Welcome to the Royal Guard, Captain Rice."

Two horns sounded a fanfare as a middle-aged couple entered the dockyard. A much younger man walked behind them. I felt certain the younger man was Prince Rupor.

"Nist," Callan said, "have our guest brought on deck."

Shortly, Raoul hobbled on deck, somewhat roughly aided by Martin. Captain Hunter's eyes widened.

"It's Bane!" Hunter shouted. "Cover him."

Half of the guards on deck leveled crossbows at Martin. Raoul let out a squeak and stopped moving.

"You've caught the man responsible for your abduction," Hunter said.

"Yes," Callan said, "but things aren't quite as you might think. Martin, turn Raoul over to Captain Hunter."

Martin propelled Raoul toward the guard captain. Raoul tried to dig in with his feet but his wounded leg buckled. Martin pulled Raoul up just as Raoul flailed his crutch for balance. The crutch struck a crossbowman's arm.

The guard's crossbow swung toward Callan, who had stepped forward to speak with Captain Hunter, and his finger jerked on the trigger.

Boost!

In terrible slow motion, I saw the crossbow string snap forward. With Callan between me and the quarrel, I couldn't deflect it or snatch it out of the air. So I did the only thing I could do. I flung Callan to the deck. The quarrel plucked her sleeve in passing. Then it struck my chest.

SHOT

I was still Boosting, so everything around me continued in slow motion.

Captain Hunter waved to his guards to lower their crossbows.

Martin pushed Raoul aside and moved toward me.

Callan looked up from the deck. Her eyes were wide and she was screaming something I couldn't quite make out.

Maybe it was the Boost distorting sounds. I didn't think Boost had ever done that to me before, but what else could it be? Then my implant canceled Boost and I felt a terrible pain in my chest.

The world returned to normal speed. Suddenly, my legs felt wobbly. Something had caused that, if I could just remember what. Oh, right— I'd been shot.

Martin caught me before my legs gave out. He lowered me to the deck and shouted "Tristan! David's been shot!"

Callan's face appeared above me. "No no no no no," she said, shaking her head with each word.

Tears rolled down her cheeks. I wanted to raise my hand and wipe away her tears but for some reason my arms weren't working.

Callan caught my head in her hands, "David, don't you dare die on me! Do you understand? That's a royal order. You're the captain of my guard and you have to obey my orders!"

From a long way away, I heard Tristan shouting, "Get out of the way! I'm a doctor! Let me through!"

To my right, I saw Raoul watching me from where he'd fallen. He smiled wide and said, "Die Rice! Die in agony!"

Martin dropped onto Raoul's chest, grabbed Raoul's throat, and began choking him while also pounding Raoul's head into the deck. I hoped that hurt.

My view was cut off as Tristan dropped to the deck next to me. He was saying something, but I couldn't hear him.

Then everything faded to black.

GO TO HER

"D avid?"

A voice came out of the darkness. It was a voice I recognized.

"Come on, lad," the voice said. "You need to pay attention."

The voice seemed to be right in front of me. I was sure my eyes were open, but I couldn't see anything.

"Enough malingering, boy!" the voice commanded. "I expect better of you than this."

"Rob?" I asked. "Is that you?"

Rob popped into view right where I thought he should be. He looked a lot better than the last time I'd seen him. His uniform was crisp with no sign of blood anywhere.

"Of course it's me, lad," Rob said. "Who else do you think they'd send to guide you?"

"But you're dead," I said. "How could anyone send you to guide anyone? Unless... Am I dead, Rob?"

"Not yet, David," Rob replied, "but you're not in very good condition. Tristan says you could go either way."

"So, are you really here or am I delusional?" I asked.

"What difference does it make?" Rob replied.

He had a point. If I died, it wouldn't matter. If I lived, I'd convince myself it was a dream.

"So, if you were sent to guide me into the afterlife, why are you here before I'm dead?" I asked.

"Remember when you came up out of the tunnels in Beloren and threw my body at Bane's men?" Rob asked.

"Yeah, about that–" I began.

"That was brilliant, David," Rob laughed. "It was almost worth dying just for that. I got to protect Callan even after I was dead."

"I'm glad you approve," I said.

"That's why I'm here before you've died, lad," Rob said. "I've been given another last chance to protect Callan."

"I don't understand," I said. "Callan isn't in danger."

"I'm not talking about physical harm, David. Callan has lost a lot of people in the last couple of weeks," Rob answered. "It's a heavy burden to have men die for you. I know, because I carried that burden myself before I died. And my death just added weight to her burden.

"You are the reason Callan's burden didn't overwhelm her," Rob continued. "Your bravery, your compassion, your dedication, and—most of all—your love eased Callan's burden."

"I just thought I fell in love with her and she with me," I said.

"You did. And she did," Rob said. "But you showed her a future beyond her burden. You showed her the way past her grief. You gave her love and she found life again. But now her new life with you is threatened. If you die, David, she may never recover."

"No. Callan is too full of vitality, too full of life for that to happen!" I insisted.

"I wouldn't be so sure of that, David. Did you know she hasn't left your side since you came out of surgery three days ago?" Rob said. "Sometimes she talks to you, sometimes she cries for you, sometimes she just sits with you. But she's always there. Always waiting for you. Listen to her, David. She's talking right now."

I concentrated. From far away, Callan's voice came to me. "Did

I ever tell you about the time Rob let me get drunk? I was sixteen and..."

My concentration broke and Callan's voice faded.

"David," Rob said, "from the moment you burst into Callan's life, you've been there for her. And now she needs you more than she's ever needed anything in her life. Go to her, lad. Be there for her again."

Rob faded from view and I found I could hear Callan quite clearly.

"...first hangover. And my last," Callan said. "Later, I realized the hangover was Rob's plan all along. Sometimes, it seemed like he was some kind of evil genius."

I opened my eyes. Callan was holding my hand, her eyes red and swollen. Tear tracks ran down her cheeks. Yet she still looked beautiful. I squeezed her hand.

"Hi honey, I'm home." I said.

"David!" Callan cried. "Oh, I was afraid I'd lost you forever."

I smiled, "No, I'll always be here for you."

BLESSING

It was another day before Tristan allowed me to have visitors —besides Callan, I mean. Tristan suggested she leave and get some rest. He even tried the old stern-doctor-issuing-orders approach. Callan let him escape with his life, but it was a close thing.

My first visitors were Callan's parents, King Edwar and Queen Elaina. Callan's mother took one look at her daughter and led her off for a bath and some food. Callan tried the same refusal that had worked so well with Tristan. Her mother just overrode it and had Callan out the door in under a minute. Tristan, who had shown them in, could only watch in stupefaction as the queen bundled Callan past him.

"How did she do that?" Tristan asked.

"I have no idea," the king replied. "I'm just glad Elaina is on my side."

As soon as Tristan left us, the king said, "Callie tells me you want to marry her."

"I do," I said.

"Why?"

"Because I love her," I replied.

"Why?"

"She's feisty," I said without hesitation.

He wasn't expecting that answer and, after a brief silence, asked, "What do you mean by that?"

I smiled, "Callan is intelligent, courageous, strong-willed, and compassionate. She can even be practical, if you yell at her loud enough."

The king said, "You left 'beautiful' off your list."

"Your Majesty, neither of us is blind," I said. "I rather thought 'beautiful' was a given."

"Yet it's the first—many times the only—thing men notice," the king said.

"If I'd met Callan at court, perhaps I'd have been like other men," I said. "Even so, possessing beauty simply makes one beautiful. Callan's other qualities make her compelling."

"Did Callie give you those answers?" King Edwar asked. He must have seen me preparing to respond because he waved me down. "No, don't answer that, David. It wasn't a serious question. But I must steer this conversation toward a different matter.

"We've been holding Prince Raoul under house arrest while we wait for King Damon to arrive from Tarteg," King Edwar said. "This whole situation is a political nightmare of colossal proportions. Callan has already told me the story, but I'd like to hear it from your perspective."

Callan and her mother returned as I was wrapping up. Callan sat next to me on the bed and rested her head on my shoulder.

"Daddy, have you finished interrogating David?" she asked.

"I'd hardly call it an interrogation," her father protested.

"David, did Daddy start off by asking why you want to marry me?" Callan said.

"Well, yes," I said.

"Interrogation," Callan pronounced. "And how did he do, Daddy dear?"

"His answers were...unexpected," King Edwar said, "and quite good."

"So we have your blessing to marry?" Callan asked.

"Would it matter if I said no?" the king growled.

"Of course not, Daddy," Callan said. "But I really do want your approval. I want you to walk me down the aisle and give me away."

"Well," the king mused, "I must admit you'd be quite a bit safer if you and your staunchest defender were sleeping together..."

I felt the heat rise in Callan's cheek as she gasped, "Daddy!"

"Blast, I didn't mean *that* and you know it," King Edwar said.

"Well, we *do* want grandchildren and an heir, Edwar," Queen Elaina said. "That's never going to happen if they don't sleep together."

"Mom!" Callan cried, hiding her face in her hands.

"Good point, Elaina," King Edwar said, "but only *after* they're married."

Callan pulled her hands from her face, "So we have your blessing?"

"Of course you have our blessing, Callie," her father smiled. He turned to me, "Welcome to the family, David."

RECOVERY

After the king and queen left, I had a steady stream of visitors. Milo, Kim, and a girl about Milo's age visited. The girl didn't say much, but she sat close to Milo and held hands with him.

After they left, I asked Callan, "Milo already has a girlfriend here at court?"

"No, it's more like he's holding auditions for the post," Callan laughed. "Milo is quite the hero around here. The guards respect the courage he showed helping us in Faroon, the pages are in awe of his accomplishments behind enemy lines, and all the younger ladies swoon and hang on his every word. His dating schedule is so complicated, I believe Kim has taken to keeping an appointment book for him."

"I hope he can keep their names straight," I said. "Hero or not, young ladies are not amused when you call them by the wrong name."

"And how would you know this?" Callan folded her arms across her chest.

"I have been to seven settled worlds besides this one," I said. "I've met my share of women and even dated a few of them. But you're the only one I've wanted to marry."

Martin entered as Callan was rewarding me with a kiss. "If I'm interrupting something, I can come back later."

"You are," I said. "Begone foul raider."

At the same time, Callan said, "Of course not, Martin. Please stay."

So Martin pulled up a chair and told me a most amazing story.

"David, did you know you have magical powers?" he asked.

"I-. What?"

"Yes, indeed. You are so pure, just being around you can cleanse the soul of the even the most foul villain," Martin said. "Yes, David, you brought the wretched raider, Martin Bane, back from the darkness with your purifying light of truth, goodness, and the Mordanian way."

"That's crazy," I said. "Who makes this stuff up?"

"No idea," Martin said, "but I added the bit about Ardhan Windslow turning my soul toward the darkness in the first place. I was just an innocent Terran Scout before his foul influence drove me to become a raider."

"Until I saved you from the darkness and all that bunk?" I asked.

"Exactly, oh shining light in my darkness," Martin laughed.

"Callan, would you hit Martin for me?"

"It's actually a useful story, darling," Callan said. "It makes it easier for some of our subjects to accept Martin's heroism in Faroon and the pardon my father granted."

"And," Martin added, "everyone wants to hear the story straight from the devil's mouth. I haven't had to pay for a drink in days."

"As long as no one asks me to make blind men see and lame beggars walk, I suppose I can live with it," I said.

We chatted for a while longer, then Martin said, "That's your third yawn in five minutes, David. Either I'm boring—which I know isn't true—or you need some rest. I'd best be going."

As he rose, I said, "One more thing, Martin. Now that you're all purified and everything, I have a request for you."

Martin hesitated a second, then said, "Name it."

"Strange as it may seem, you're the best friend I've got on this planet. Scratch that. You're the best friend I've got on any planet. Would you be the best man in our wedding?"

For the second time since I'd met him, Martin Bane was at a loss for words. After several attempts to speak, he just nodded.

AS ONE

The next day, King Damon of Tarteg arrived. The situation had been tense enough with just Prince Rupor around. It got worse with his father on hand. Prince Raoul was released into his father's custody, but he was restricted to the chambers set aside for visiting royalty.

For once, I was happy to be restricted to bed rest. It allowed me to avoid most of the difficult diplomatic wrangling. Not even doctor's orders could save me from being called upon to tell my tale to King Damon. He was escorted to my room and spent three hours grilling me. No detail escaped his notice and I was exhausted by the time he was finished with me.

"Do you think he believes us?" I asked Callan when we were alone.

"Yes," she answered. "He wishes he didn't and who can blame him? But he knows Queen Beatrice and he knows Raoul."

"What about Rupor? How is he taking all of this?"

"I think Rupor is embarrassed and ashamed of Raoul," she said. "Rupor is also not very fond of you. I think it has something to do with stealing his woman. According to Milo, the Tartegian royal guards are upset, too. He says they were looking forward to watching my backside."

Callan heaved a theatrical sigh and wiggled her backside, "When the Tartegians leave, who will I get to watch my backside?"

A slight gurgling sound came from the door. Tristan was standing in the doorway, his eyes wide and his face red.

"It appears Tristan is already watching it," I said. "Problem solved."

Tristan turned brighter red, "You seem to have survived your royal interview in fine fettle." Backing out of the room, he said, "Well done, my boy."

Callan collapsed into my arms and we laughed long and hard.

The next day, the Tartegian delegation left. Raoul would be given an airship and sent into exile. Queen Beatrice was to spend the rest of her days in a convent. Callan and I were just glad to put the whole affair behind us.

The day after that, Tristan allowed me to get up and walk. Callan was there, helping and encouraging me. A short walk left me gasping, but I had begun to hate lying around in bed. I pushed myself hard to make sure I was ready for the wedding and all of the festivities that would follow the ceremony.

Five weeks after I was shot, I stood next to Martin before the gathered nobility of a dozen countries. My heart was hammering as the cathedral doors were thrown open and I beheld my bride. Callan was radiant, more beautiful than I could ever have imagined. I'm told her father looked splendid, as well. I never even noticed him.

The ceremony passed in a blur. We gave our vows and had our first kiss as husband and wife. Then it was down the aisle and into a waiting carriage. We paraded through the streets of Morda, cheered by thousands of subjects who had turned out to see their beloved princess and her new husband. At the end of the parade was the wedding reception, with dancing and dining.

It was late before we were allowed to escape the festivities. An honor guard, led by Captain Hunter, escorted us to our chambers. Captain Hunter held the door as I carried Callan across the threshold and closed it once we were inside. At long last, we were alone.

We fell into each other's arms, time went away, and we were as one.

THE STORY CONTINUES...

David's and Callan's story continues in *Scout's Oath*.
Available now!

If you enjoyed *Scout's Honor*, please post a brief review.
Reader recommendations are the best advertising.

ABOUT THE AUTHOR

 Growing up, Henry worked at the usual range of menial jobs before ending up in software development. In between the menial jobs and the IT jobs, he achieved some small fame as the writer and co-creator of the small press comic book titles Southern Knights and X-Thieves. In 2006, Henry also took up the mantle of professional storyteller. He performs regularly throughout the state of North Carolina and has recently released his first book of children's stories.

Henry has been a fan of science fiction for as long as he can remember. He has loved space opera and planetary romance since the beginning, that is why his science fiction novels end up in those subgenres.

Henry currently lives in Raleigh, NC, with his wife, son, two cats, and lots of imaginary friends all clamoring to tell him of their adventures.

www.henryvogelwrites.com

ALSO BY HENRY VOGEL